THE KARAOKE QUEEN

And Her Year of Yes

Annie Powers

ISBN: 0692749047
ISBN 13: 9780692749043
Library of Congress Control Number: 2016910673
AnniePowers, Nashville, TN

SOUNDTRACK TO THE BOOK

1. Silver Lining- Rilo Kiley
2. January Hymn- the Decemberist
3. Look at Miss Ohio- Gillian Welch
4. I Told You I Was Mean- Elle King
5. Love Song- Sara Bareilles
6. February- OK Go
7. To Make You Feel My Love- Adele
8. Bad Romance- Lady Gaga
9. Girls Just Want to Have fun- Cyndi Lauper
10. The Waters of March- Sofia
11. Skinny Love- Birdy
12. April Come She Will- Simon and Garfunkel
13. Summer Wind- Frank Sinatra
14. Born to Run- Bruce Springsteen
15. Pontoon- Little Big Town
16. On a Boat- The Lonely Island Ft. T-Pain

17. Sit Still, Look Pretty- Daya
18. September-Earth wind and Fire
19. I Need a Lover-John Cougar Mellencamp
20. Rumor Has It- Adele
21. October road- James Taylor
22. I Will Always Love You- Whitney Houston
23. Superficial Love- Ruth B
24. November Blue- The Avett Brothers
25. Kocaine Karolina- Elle King
26. December- Norah Jones
27. Rise to The Sun- Alabama Shakes

Follow:
Spotify Playlist: Karaoke Queen-Year of Yes
Spotify Member Name: **KARAOKEQUEENAP**

PROLOGUE

Kennedy gently jostled the tiny puppies up and down. She stared into their adorable puppy eyes. She smelled their delicious puppy breath and cuddled their black and tan curly fluffiness. This was going to be a very tough decision.

"They're both so adorable!" Kennedy said befuddled. "It's too hard to decide! I want them both!" she said.

"One of them is going to another family. You can't have both," said the breeder. Kennedy could tell that the breeder was becoming annoyed by Kennedy's enthusiasm.

"I didn't mean it. I don't have enough money for both, anyways," replied Kennedy. She lifted up the feisty one in her left hand. "You are my new best friend," she said to the tiny puppy in her hand.

"I'm going to take the fat one. She seems like a survivor," Kennedy said.

It had been a gray and misty day in mid-December when Kennedy had made the hour-long drive to pick up her new puppy on a farm in eastern North Carolina. One of her patients had recommended this dog breeder to her. Kennedy and her fiancé, Sam, had put their name on a puppy waiting list five months beforehand. She had been waiting for this day for a long time.

Kennedy's new puppy was only forty-seven days old when she picked her up. That was how old the book *The Family Dog* recommended the dog should be in order to gain a great bond with its owner. Kennedy had done all the puppy research and preparation she needed. She was ready.

Kennedy put the puppy in its designated car seat in the passenger side of the car and shut the door. But as soon as she climbed into the driver's seat, the puppy started whining and yelping loudly. Kennedy felt a sudden twinge of guilt at taking a puppy from its mother. She fought back tears as she pulled her car out of the long dirt driveway and took a right turn in the direction she had come. The breeder had convinced her that the mother dog was ready for her puppies to leave her. She had said the mother was tired of them pestering her. After hearing this little puppy's cries, though, Kennedy was skeptical.

She drove a little farther down the gravel road, and the rain started beating heavily on the car. Suddenly she was at a fork in the road, two paths before her. She could not remember from which way she had come. The puppy was crying louder, and her GPS was not working. This was a nightmare. This farm was not on Google Maps yet. She was frustrated, and so was the whimpering puppy.

After a few moments, an SUV pulled up next to her.

"Are you lost?" yelled the woman from the vehicle in a thick southern accent. The puppy yelped even louder as the rain beat down even harder on the car.

"Yes. I need to get back to the main road so I can get my GPS to work," said Kennedy, a tear running down her cheek.

"Did you just pick up that puppy from Shirley?" the friendly stranger asked.

"Yes. I don't know how to make her stop crying!" yelled Kennedy over the loud rain.

"Try holding her in your lap. Puppies like to be warm."

Kennedy picked up the three-pound puppy and placed her on her lap. The puppy instantly stopped crying. Then the woman was kind enough to point her in the direction she needed to go. They were on the road again.

"Let's see—what should we name you?" Kennedy asked the now sleeping puppy in her lap. She had made a list of names. Yet she was still undecided. So she started calling out the names while she drove.

"Roxie...Lucy...Stella!" she yelled. The puppy didn't move.

"Rosie!" As soon as Kennedy said Rosie, the little puppy's head and ears perked up, and it gave a little bark.

"Rosie it is," said Kennedy.

When Kennedy finally made it back to their apartment, she wrapped the puppy in a towel and placed it on her bed. For the next three hours, Rosie slept or watched as Kennedy packed most of her belongings, at least all that she could fit into her four-door sedan. She left behind all of her bedroom furniture, decorations anything that wouldn't fit or could be replaced. Then she left the ring on his bedroom dresser with a note.

> Dear Sam,
> I'm thankful for the years that I spent with you, for everything that we shared, and for every chance we had to grow. I'll take the best memories of us with me. This wasn't exactly what I wanted, but I know it's for the best. Maybe it's because I look at everything as a lesson, or because I don't want to walk around angry, or maybe it's because I finally understand. There are things we don't want to happen but have to accept, things we don't want to know but have to learn, and people we can't live without but have to let go.
>
> Thank you for your kindness and understanding.
> Kennedy
> PS The ring should be on top of this note.

Kennedy had stolen most of her letter from the dialogue of a *Criminal Minds* episode that she had just watched (the one where JJ is reassigned to another department).

She meant a lot of it and thought it was very fitting. But the truth was, Kennedy had fallen out of love with Sam. She knew she might look back on all of the good memories they'd had together. But she also knew that she could never go back. Too many things had happened, and too many things had changed. Ultimately, she was relieved that they hadn't gone through with the marriage.

"It's just you and me now, pup," Kennedy told Rosie.

Then Rosie and Kennedy began their three-day trek back to the Natural State, where Kennedy hadn't lived in several years.

And the grass it was a ticking,
And the sun was on the rise.
I never felt so wicked
As when I willed our love to die.

—Rilo Kiley

1. JANUARY

What were the words I meant to say before you left?
When I could see your breath lead where you were going to.
Maybe I should just let it be, and maybe it will all come back to me.
Sing, oh, January, oh.

—*The Decemberists*

SOUTHERN FAMILY

"This is not how it was supposed to go," said Josh, Kennedy's younger brother. They were sitting around the dinner table at Kennedy's parents' house. "You're supposed to have a husband first. Then y'all get a puppy together," he said.

"That's not true at all," said Kennedy. "Plenty of single women have dogs—and even children, for that matter."

"But now, if you date someone again, they have to like you and your dog," said Josh.

"That makes it so much more difficult."

"If they don't like Rosie, then they aren't worth it," said Kennedy.

"I can't tell you if I know any single men in Little Rock," said Brianna, Josh's wife.

"Most of the people I know there that are your age are married. It's going to be hard dating there," she said.

"I'm only twenty-seven. I'm a dentist. I'll figure it out," said Kennedy.

Kennedy was five foot seven, with a slender frame and pale skin that turned a mottled red when she was embarrassed or angry. She rarely wore makeup and constantly surprised her patients, coworkers, bartenders, parents etc. who could not believe she was 27. She would describe her caramel colored blonde hair as unruly and unmanageable, but others would marvel at her lustrous curls that bounced as she walked. And anyone who met her could not help but comment on her beautiful large gray-blue eyes.

She loved her loud, noisy, opinionated family. She was a lot like them, but more serious and not as loud. She loved to tell jokes, laugh, and play card games at holidays. She was the only girl with two younger brothers. Her youngest brother, Robert, was in medical school in St. Louis. Her other brother, Josh, lived in Dallas, Texas with his wife.

Her childhood was a happy one. Kennedy went to Catholic school, had plenty of friends and a huge extended family on both her mom and dad's side. However, Kennedy also yearned for more adventure beyond what her large family and home life could provide.

"I just wish you would have given Sam more of a chance, Kennedy. We all loved him so much," said Kennedy's mom.

"Mom, you know that I wasn't happy living there. Sam and I both would have been miserable if I had stayed," said Kennedy.

"I just hope you don't regret your decision," said Josh. "Because I don't think he'll take you back."

"I don't want him to take me back. I don't plan on going back. I did this for me and only me," said Kennedy. "Rosie and I will be just fine without him."

LEARNING TO SAY YES

Kennedy got off work early Friday to pick Bailey up from the airport. Bailey was flying in from Atlanta and Kennedy was incredibly excited to see her. She had been one of Kennedy's best friends in dental school. Also, Bailey's ex-boyfriend, Sean, was best friends with Sam, Kennedy's ex-fiancé. Bailey, a petite brunette with tan skin and dark brown eyes, was a native of Georgia. She had settled in Atlanta after graduating dental school. It had been about seven months since the friends had seen each other. The two women had a lot of catching up to do.

"It's strange to say it, Kennedy, but you seem like you're so much happier here," Bailey told Kennedy as they sat down to dinner.

"Thanks, Bay! Well, technically, I've lived here for two weeks. Maybe I'm just happier because I've moved."

"Yes, maybe that's it. It seems like you're glowing! What was that like in North Carolina with Sam? I've hardly talked to you since you moved there."

"North Carolina was difficult for me. His family was really nice; don't get me wrong. But I didn't fit in with them. I felt like an outsider. Also, he changed from when we were in school. He wanted me to be someone that I wasn't. There were several factors. In the end, there were more cons than pros of us staying together."

"Well, I'm glad you at least moved there and figured this out before you guys got married," said Bailey. "Now you don't have to spend the rest of your life wondering what it would have been like if you had stayed there."

"Yes, me too. I will never regret moving there. But I will also never regret moving away. So, are you and Sean still on friendly terms?"

"Yes, we keep in touch. It's really hard not to when we're in the same profession and live in the same town. But I'm dating Aaron now. He's such a great guy. We're the same religion, and we went to the same undergrad. It's just so much easier to date Aaron. There's a lot less drama with him than there was with Sean. To be honest, though, if Sean had proposed, I would have said yes. Also, I don't know if I would have been brave enough to cancel a wedding," said Bailey.

"You're right. It was hard to stop it. The truth is, we most likely would have gotten divorced shortly after the wedding. That, or I would have gotten really depressed and died an early death from bingeing on ice cream and fruit snacks. I understand now how people get divorced after a wedding. It's so easy to ignore the red flags and keep on planning the wedding of your dreams. Wedding plans are like a giant snowball, just building momentum as they roll down a hill."

"How far along were your wedding plans?" asked Bailey.

"I had deposits on the church and the reception. Also, I still have my wedding dress."

"I hope you didn't lose a lot of money."

"It wasn't too bad. The reception was at a public park pavilion that was relatively inexpensive. Also, the church was free. I think just the money for the rehearsal dinner was lost. His parents paid for that," said Kennedy.

"What are you going to do with the dress?"

"I'm not sure yet. My grandma bought it for me. She still insists that I wear it when I actually do get married."

"Would that be weird? Did you think about him when you bought the dress?"

"At this point, I don't think it would be strange. You can have the right wedding dress but the wrong guy. Also, my grandma told me that the dress will probably turn yellow before I find a man to settle down with."

"No! She said that!" Bailey said, laughing, almost choking on her salmon.

"Yes. She's intent on me wearing that dress. She spent a lot of money on it. I love that dress, and I will wear it if I can."

"That's good. Just don't tell the man you marry that you already had it picked out. What happened to the ring? Did you give it back, or did you keep it?" asked Bailey.

"I gave it back to him. I felt like I was the one leaving him. He deserved to have it back. It was such a beautiful ring! I have dreams about that ring." Kennedy sighed.

"You know what you need?"

"What?"

"You need to do a year of yes."

"A year of yes?" said Kennedy. "That sounds a little bit flamboyant and dangerous."

"My friend Courtney in Atlanta did it after one of her big breakups. Also, Shonda Rhimes wrote a book about it. You need a year in which you say yes to things that you wouldn't normally say yes to. This will get you out of your comfort zone," said Bailey.

"So, I am supposed to just say yes to everything? This sounds like a trick. You know that I could possibly end up getting arrested or getting a sexually transmitted disease or dying if I do this, right?" Kennedy laughed.

"How about you say yes—but within reason?"

"Year of yes...Y-O-Y...I think I could work on that. I'll see how much trouble I can get into—within reason." Kennedy smiled.

THE NINER

After dinner, the girls walked past a bar called the Afterthought. There was a band playing Kennedy's favorite song of the moment. The bar charged a ten-dollar cover at the door, but Bailey sweet-talked the doorman into letting them in for free. The band had just begun playing the song *Look At Miss Ohio*:

> *He's got his arm around her shoulder,*
> *A regimental soldier, and Mama starts pushing the wedding gown.*
> *She says I wanna do right, but not right now.*

Kennedy swayed to the music as Bailey talked to a cute lawyer at the bar. The crowd was mostly older people, and he looked like one of the youngest guys there. He was probably in his mid-thirties. Kennedy wanted to go where there were more people her age. So after the song was over, Kennedy grabbed Bailey from her lawyer, and they headed to Ciao Baci.

"The men here are so nice!" said Bailey.

"You've only met one," said Kennedy.

"In Atlanta, most of the men only want to get into your pants. I mean, there are guys that are in their late thirties that are like 'maybe one day I'll settle down.' That man seemed to actually care about what I did for a living. I felt like he wanted to get to know me! He was definitely looking for a serious relationship. You should have met him!"

"It's too bad you're dating what's his name. Also, I wasn't that attracted to him. What's he doing wearing a three-piece suit at a bar on a Friday night?" said Kennedy.

"Picky, picky! Don't be jealous because he found me first!" Bailey laughed.

Kennedy met Bryan—or, as Bailey would later call him, Niner—at the little house restaurant and bar Ciao Baci. Bailey and Kennedy were sharing stories over drinks when Bryan came up to their table and asked if he could borrow a chair. He told the girls that his brother was coming to join him and he needed another seat.

Instead of taking the extra seat, Bryan sat down at the table and introduced himself. He was a striking man with a southern accent, short thick brown hair and a five o'clock shadow. He told the girls that he was an electrical engineer from Memphis. He had moved to Little Rock two years ago when his brother got into law school there.

Bryan was a very expressive talker. He liked to talk with his hands while telling stories. Kennedy watched his hands move fluidly and realized that he was missing his pinky finger on his right hand.

Kennedy was straightforward and asked him, "How did you lose your pinky finger?"

"Oh, this?" he said, holding up his nub of a pinky. "I was at Lake Hamilton on a boat with some buddies of mine. I was drunk and getting off the boat into the water. I had a ring on my pinky finger. The boat had a ladder that folded out into the water. My pinky finger was pinched between the boat and the ladder. I tried to pull it out instead of lifting up the ladder. So I pulled my pinky off," Bryan said casually and without concern. He had obviously told this story many times.

Both of the girls looked at each other and cringed.

"I can't imagine how much that hurt," said Bailey. "How did they get you treated if you were at the lake?"

"They called a helicopter rescue team to come and get me. I was very drunk. I don't remember it hurting that badly," replied Bryan.

"Did they try to save the finger?" asked Kennedy.

"No. By the time they got there, they said my finger was too far gone."

Already Kennedy could tell that this man was reckless. However, when he asked for her number later that night, she gave it to him willingly.

After all, this was the Year of Yes.

Kennedy was on her third date with Bryan when she realized that he wasn't the one for her. The first two dates, he had taken her to nice dinners, and they had had a great time. They had had a couple of make-out sessions on the doorstep of her townhouse. But Kennedy didn't think she was ready to sleep with him. It might have been that she hadn't slept with anyone but Sam in four years. Or the fact that she thought something was off about Bryan.

"I have something I want to tell you," Kennedy told Bryan while they were drinking cocktails at Bar Louie in west Little Rock.

"Go ahead," replied Bryan.

"I was engaged before I moved here."

"Oh, I see. How long ago was the breakup?"

"Two months ago."

"Oh, that wasn't too long ago. How long did you date?"

"Four years," replied Kennedy.

"That sucks. Did he cheat on you?"

"No. We just realized that we had irreconcilable differences."

"Oh, well, I can be your fallback guy. I don't mind. Girls always need a guy to fall back on," said Bryan with a wink.

"Wait, what? Girls don't always need guys to fall back on."

"Yeah. I mean, most girls after a breakup have guys waiting in the wings. You know, so they won't be alone. They need to have someone to support them."

"I can support myself just fine, thank you! I'm doing things successfully without a man in my life," said Kennedy as though she was still trying to convince herself.

"When my ex-girlfriend broke up with me, she had a guy waiting to date her. However, it just happened to be my best friend. That's why I moved to Little Rock with my brother," said Bryan.

"I hate to tell you this, Bryan, but she was probably already sleeping with him while you were dating her. Also, not all women are the same," said Kennedy.

Bryan sighed.

"I've been trying to tell myself this entire time that that wasn't true. But I guess it's possible that they were sleeping together when I was dating her. She was one of those really hot Hawaiian Tropics models," said Bryan. "She was so hot." He sighed again and then smiled to himself.

"Anyways," Kennedy said, rolling her eyes, "are those the girls that have orange spray tans and do bathing-suit competitions?"

"Those are the ones!" said Bryan.

"Well, good for her for having the confidence and the body."

The later they stayed at Bar Louie, the more intoxicated they became. Also, the more Kennedy realized she did not have anything in common with this guy. They shared stories from their past and talked about how they had grown up. Then something possessed Bryan to tell Kennedy that he used cocaine on a regular basis. This was a red flag. Regular cocaine use was definitely on her list of deal breakers. Kennedy secretly wondered if Bryan had been on cocaine when he lost his finger. She'd had friends in college who did cocaine. However, she didn't plan on dating anyone with an addictive personality. Even during the YOY.

At the end of the date, Kennedy told Bryan that she didn't think she could see him again. She told him that she wasn't into a relationship right now, since she had just gotten out of a serious relationship. She didn't need him to fall back on.

It turned out Kennedy was right about the addictive personality. Bryan called and texted her every day for the next four weeks. He added, deleted, and re-added her on Facebook, over and over again. One day he showed up at her house, uninvited, with flowers in his hands. Kennedy did not open the door. She called her elderly neighbor and asked her to stick her head out the door and yell, "She's not home!" Then he stopped calling and texting. Maybe he found someone else, maybe he saw her out with other guys. It didn't really matter to Kennedy that he slowly faded away.

I know you still bother,
Because love is for the poor.
So cut out your knocking,
'Cause I will never come.
I will never come to the door.

—*Elle King*

INTRO TO KARAOKE

The last Tuesday in January, Kennedy went on her first blind date. He was a friend with the boyfriend of a dental hygienist that worked closely with Kennedy. The blind date's name was Nick Sharp. He was the epitome of a southern gentleman. He was also rugged-looking with dark hair and eyes broad shoulders that tapered to a slim waist. He had a degree in emergency management. However, currently he was doing light jobs in construction.

Nick asked Kennedy what she liked to do for fun. She told him dancing, trivia, and karaoke.

"Have you been to Town Pump yet?" asked Nick over the phone.

"No, I've never heard of Town Pump," said Kennedy.

"It's a local dive bar. It's famous for karaoke on the first Friday of every month and every Tuesday. Let's go to dinner and then to Town Pump."

"It's a plan," said Kennedy.

Considering it was a Tuesday night, Town Pump was packed. People of all ages and backgrounds were waiting to sing at this hole-in-the-wall bar.

"That stage is intimidating," Kennedy told Nick.

"Yeah, I would never go up there by myself. Heck, I don't even plan on going up there at all. Are you good at singing, or do you just like to watch people sing?"

"I'm sometimes good at singing. I mainly like to sing in my car. I think it's all about confidence. You have to be incredibly confident in the fact that you are subjecting the audience to your mediocre singing voice," said Kennedy.

"Well, let's hear that confidence."

Kennedy requested "Love Song" by Sara Bareilles. Her name was called almost immediately after she put her name on the list. She had not psyched herself up for this one. In fact, she hadn't even ordered a drink yet. She was not ready. But it was the year of yes, right?

She stepped on stage and timidly began singing. Her hands and her voice were shaking ferociously. This was embarrassing. The karaoke DJ on the side of the stage grabbed an extra microphone and started to sing backup to help her out. *Bless him*, she thought.

Kennedy walked off the stage, head down and red-faced. She knew that she could do better than that. She sang all the time in the car and she had a pretty good voice. She had not been courageous enough. This was something she was going to tackle in the Year of Yes. *Yes to being better at karaoke*, she told herself.

Nick walked her out to the car and gave her a kiss good-night. His breath smelled as if he had halitosis. Kennedy had been pretending that this didn't exist all night. However, the dentist in her couldn't help but suggest that he come in for an office visit. He was too handsome for her not to consider going on another date.

2. FEBRUARY

*In your fitted raincoat and tangled
winter hair,
Cheeks a little rosy in the February air,
And running through the subway to catch the
uptown train,
Spend the night just dancing.*

—OK Go

SOUTH AND THE CITY

"Make sure you wear a hat while you're walking around the city," said Judy, Kennedy's mom, over the phone. Kennedy was on a layover in Charlotte waiting for a flight to New York City. Jenna, her friend from dental school had called her in January and invited her to come visit for the weekend. Kennedy, who was still paying off her school loans had booked the cheapest flight she could find.

"Why a hat?" Kennedy asked.

"Because I saw on the news that there was a man who was pledging allegiance to Isis, running around New York City, and hitting people in the head with a hammer," said Judy.

"So you want me to wear a hat and not a helmet?"

"The hat will deter the guy with the hammer."

"There are millions of people in New York, Mom. Hopefully, the odds are in my favor, and I will not get hit on the head with a hammer. You can't just plan for those things."

"Just be careful! I love you!"

"Love you too, Mom," Kennedy said and hung up the phone shaking her head.

Also on her layover, Kennedy had a text-message conversation with Nick that made her not want to talk to him again.

Nick: Hey! What are you doing this weekend?

Kennedy: I'm flying to New York City to see one of my friends from dental school.

Nick: Oh, by yourself?

Kennedy: Yes.

Nick: So you think you can just fly around to different cities all by yourself?

Kennedy: What? Why is this a question?

Nick: I don't think it's safe for a young woman to travel alone.

Kennedy: Well, I think it is.

Kennedy: Also

(...)

Kennedy put her phone down in her lap and looked around the terminal, thinking about how to let Nick know that she didn't appreciate his chauvinism.

Then she texted him: I do what I want.

Kennedy had been to New York City before. But she had never travelled there alone. She was excited about it. It had occurred to her that large cities could be dangerous, but she didn't let her mind get away from her like Nick and her mom were. She wasn't going to let Nick change her mind about traveling alone.

Kennedy took a taxi from the airport to Jenna's apartment. Jenna was originally from Missouri and upon graduation, landed not one but two jobs in New York. She worked at two different offices about 2 miles apart in upper Manhattan. She was a tall green-eyed red head who almost always wore her long straight hair in a ponytail. Jenna was already out eating dinner with friends. Kennedy dropped her luggage with the doorman at Jenna's apartment and then took the same cab to meet Jenna who had a bowl of ice cream and a beer waiting for her at the bar. Jenna was there with her friend Lauren, who was also a dentist in New York. Lauren was from upstate New York but had been in the city for almost two years and knew how to navigate it with ease.

"Ice cream and beer! Two of my favorite things! You're amazing!" said Kennedy.

"I know you too well," said Jenna.

"We're going to karaoke tonight. Does that sound good?" asked Jenna.

"Karaoke sounds like a good idea," Kennedy replied with some reserve. She was still nursing her wounds from her embarrassing performance at Town Pump.

"Awesome. We're going to Keats. I heard that the cast of *Glee* frequents this karaoke place!" said Jenna.

The girls tabbed out and walked to Fifty-Fifth and Eighth Street, where they met up with Jenna's friend James at Keats. He had a table waiting for them. James was another young dentist living in New York. He was there with his boyfriend of the moment, Marcus.

At the bar, James helped Kennedy set up an OkCupid account and the Tinder app on her phone. At the time, they were the two most popular dating apps in the city.

"I met Marcus on this app! I love it!" said James.

"There are so many men on here," said Kennedy as she swiped through thousands of photos of men. "I just got five messages, and I've been on it less than five minutes. How do you choose?"

"It's overwhelming dating here—at first. Then, the longer you live here, the easier it is. You just kind of run through them and figure out what you want," said James.

"Watch out for creepers," said Jenna. "A guy that I matched with the other day sent me a message that just said, 'I want to lick you.' I was like, 'Ew.' By the way, I'm singing 'Bad Romance' by Lady Gaga!"

Kennedy thought everyone at this karaoke bar was aspiring to be the next famous musician/singer. There were some amazing singers in the bar. Kennedy put her favorite song sung like Adele, but by Bob Dylan "To Make You Feel My Love."

Kennedy put her song in at ten o'clock. At midnight, she didn't think she would ever get to sing. Then a Cyndi

Lauper song came up in the queue, and whoever was supposed to sing it had not shown up. Jenna grabbed her by the wrist. "I love this song! We're getting up onstage to sing it!" she yelled.

Kennedy and Jenna grabbed the microphones and started the song:

Some boys take a beautiful girl
And hide her away from the rest of the world.
I want to be the one to walk in the sun.
Oh girls, they want to have fun!

Three large women jumped up on the stage and started dancing like Cyndi Lauper around Jenna and Kennedy. Lauren and James laughed and took videos of the shenanigans. Marcus got up on stage and started dancing with the women. For the moment, it was much better than the Bob Dylan song Kennedy was going to sing.

It was three in the morning when the group of dentists drunkenly meandered back to Jenna and Lauren's place in Koreatown. To Kennedy, it felt like midnight. One night in New York City had felt like an entire week in Arkansas.

"Are you running the half marathon on Sunday?" asked Lauren.

"Wait, what? You guys are running a half marathon on Sunday?" asked Kennedy.

"Yes! It's in Central Park. You should run it with us!" said Jenna.

"Do I look like Wonder Woman? I know I'm supposed to say yes. But I feel like this one is peer pressure, or a joke. I've run two 5Ks in my life. The last one I ran, I watched as another dentist --one who had just retired —run past me at a snail's pace across the finish line. I'm a horrible runner."

"Do it! I'll run with you. My foot has been hurting lately. So we can mosey along the half," said Jenna.

"It'll probably take all day. I might miss my flight. But okay," Kennedy replied skeptically. *Was a half marathon within reason?* Kennedy asked herself.

The next day Jenna and Lauren both worked a half-day at their respective jobs. In New York City, dentists work on Saturdays and sometimes even on Sundays. This amazed Kennedy. In the South, everything shut down on Sunday. She would never dream of working on a Sunday.

Kennedy took the day to wander the city alone. She grabbed a bagel and took the subway to 30 Rockefeller Plaza, as Lauren had suggested. This was Kennedy's first subway ride alone in New York City. Her sweet southern grandmother would be thoroughly disappointed in her for riding the subway alone. In the crowded subway car, she watched a homeless man read out loud from a book he was holding upside down.

It was cold and windy on the top of the Rock viewing deck. She met a group of friendly French tourists on the way up. Employing her college French classes, she struck up a conversation with the group. She had her new friends take photos of her pretending that she was touching the top of the Empire State Building. Then she gladly took photos of them on the deck. After that, she moseyed down to the NBC studio's gift shop.

"Hey, do you want to be part of a live audience screening for *The Tonight Show*?" asked a girl sitting on the stairs in the gift shop.

"Yes, that sounds like fun. When does it start?" asked Kennedy.

"Thirty minutes," said the girl.

Kennedy watched Jimmy Fallon shoot a live audience promo for *The Tonight Show*. It was the most exciting thing she had done yet in the Year of Yes. Fallon was just starting his run as host for *The Tonight Show*. *Where would I be at this moment if I hadn't said yes?* Kennedy wondered.

HALF OF A HALF

After Jenna and Lauren got off work and Kennedy was done ogling Jimmy Fallon from a distance, the girls met up at a Nike store to sign up for the race on Sunday. Kennedy thought this might be the dumbest thing she had done so far in her Year of Yes. Her ex-fiancé, Sam, had always made fun of the fact that she couldn't run. It was on the list of things that his ideal wife should be able to do—run with him.

Kennedy had been running a lot more since she moved to Little Rock. After work, she would run about a mile with Rosie two to three times a week. It was a way for her to work out and exhaust the hyper puppy at the same time. However, a mile was not going to cut it this time. Also, she always got hives while running. Kennedy made sure she had antihistamines to take before this race.

Kennedy purchased an armband and ear buds to hold her iPhone while she ran. She bought new running pants and socks. Luckily, she had brought her tennis shoes and a sports bra and tank top.

The race, called Women Now, inspired women to get out, run, and, apparently, change the world while running. Kennedy thought the message was inspiring. However, she felt the race was poorly organized and expensive. The sign-up fee was ninety dollars a person. There was no mention in the marketing materials of any of the money going to charity. Also, the shirts they received in their gift bags were poorly made, ruched down the back, and clearly not designed to complement any woman's body. *Was this race organized by a man?* She thought.

At seven o'clock Sunday morning, Central Park was crowded with thousands of women in running gear. Hoda Kotb, a co-host on the Today Show, was running the race as well. They were filming part of it for her morning talk show before the race. The three young dentists watched as Hoda gave an inspirational speech to the runners. Jenna made joke about how Hoda had to put her wine glass down to run the half marathon.

Jenna and Kennedy were in the slow group. Lauren was up front, running with the fast group. Jenna and Kennedy jogged along slowly while they watched thin and incredibly fit women fly past them. They would run fast down the downhills and walk fast up the hills. The girls talked the entire time they were walking/running. They were talking about patient care and Jenna's dating life in New York.

When it came time to circle around Central Park for the second time, the girls were talking while they were running, and they became distracted. Somehow, they managed to get in the wrong lane with a large group of women. These women were the runners who had already passed them and were on their second lap. Kennedy and Jenna suddenly found themselves headed to the finish line early and by accident. Quickly, they tried to turn around, but it wasn't possible. They were surrounded by women running in the opposite direction and in a small space.

Everyone on the sidelines was cheering and clapping for the runners finishing the race around them. Kennedy felt like a fraud. They were surrounded by women who had worked so hard to train for this and every half marathon they had ever run. These women were all sweating and some were clearly in pain. They had made an awesome time on their half marathon. But Kennedy and Jenna had only run half of a half marathon.

The volunteers at the finish line gave each woman a blanket to wrap around herself to cool down, and there was food available as well.

"Congratulations, ladies! You made such great time! Let me take your photo!" said one of the race photographers. Kennedy and Jenna laughed the entire time their pictures were being taken, holding up their medals. Then they walked around the park waiting for Lauren to finish her race. In the end, Kennedy had only said yes to half of a half marathon. She still posted the picture of Jenna and her finishing the race on Instagram. She secretly wanted Sam to see it.

Watch me run without you.

THE PILOT

One of Kennedy's best friends, Sydney, was coming to stay with Kennedy in Little Rock again. Sydney was a traveling nurse. At five feet two inches tall and 102 pounds, Sydney was tiny. The traces of the college girl lingered in Sydney's smile and the thinness of her body. On her brown skin was just the right hint of make-up, enough to show she wasn't a kid but not so much as an older woman would wear. Her bags were constantly packed and her everyday attire consisted of a comfortable well ironed pair of scrubs. Technically, she lived with her boyfriend, Trey, in Denver. But she spent a lot of time working in several different clinics around the country.

Sydney found her seat on the plane. She was in the window seat next to a tall man who was already falling asleep. She thought this was great. She didn't like talking to people on planes. She liked reading her magazine in peace.

Sydney and Kennedy had known each other since the first grade. That had been twenty-two years ago. They had been through a lot together. Sydney was going to be a bridesmaid in Kennedy's wedding. She still had a wineglass hanging in her kitchen that said Maid of Honor on it. Maybe one day, she hoped, Kennedy would be a bridesmaid in her Sydney's wedding to Trey.

Sydney had been waiting on Trey to propose for a few months now. She had moved to Denver to be with him while he was completing his residency training in oncology. She felt that she had taken a risk moving for him, and she was getting anxious about planning the rest of her—or their—life together.

The man next to her on the plane was snoring lightly. He was a tall, broad-shouldered man with dark brown curly hair high cheekbones and tanned skin. He looked as if he was in his early thirties. Sydney was amazed at his ability to fall asleep even before the plane left the runway.

An hour into the flight, Sydney was reading an article about healthy eating habits for daily living in *Women's Health* magazine when she felt the man beside her slowly falling onto the right side of her head and shoulder.

This man was a giant. If he had fallen on her any faster, he might be broken one of her limbs. Sydney used both of her arms to push and shake the sleeping stranger.

"Wake up! You're squishing me!" yelled Sydney, as quietly as possible. She didn't want to cause a scene.

The startled stranger jumped back and straightened up. His large brown eyes were wide open, and his glasses were crooked. He seemed surprised he was still buckled into the seat.

"I'm sorry; I didn't realize I had fallen asleep," said the young man as he went to adjust his glasses.

"It's okay that you were sleeping, but you were about to crush me," said Sydney.

"Again, I apologize completely," said the man.

"Did you take a Dramamine? I've never seen anyone sleep that soundly on a plane. Do you not like flying?" asked Sydney.

"Yes, I hate flying," said the stranger very quickly and then laughed sarcastically. "Actually, I'm a pilot, so that wouldn't go over well," he said.

"You're a pilot? Where's your uniform?"

"I'm in the air force. I fly C-130s. The carriers. The J model. It's basically like a taxicab in the sky for the military. My name is David, by the way." He stuck out his hand for Sydney to shake.

"I'm Sydney. Why are you flying to Little Rock?"

"Actually, I'm stationed at the Little Rock Air Force base. I was visiting my parents in Colorado. What are you doing in Little Rock?"

"I'm from northwest Arkansas, but I live in Denver now. I'm a traveling nurse. I've been sent to Little Rock a lot lately. Luckily, I have friends and family who live here."

"Traveling nurse sounds like a fun job," said David.

"Yes, it is. It gets a little exhausting, and I have long hours. But it's worth the sacrifice. I'm working toward becoming a nurse practitioner."

"That's really cool," said David. "Looks like the plane is about to land."

"I always get nervous on landings," said Sydney.

"I wouldn't worry too much. It basically lands itself," said David.

The two strangers went quiet while the plane was landing. Sydney always thought it was awkward to talk to people on planes, although this man was incredibly interesting and handsome as well.

When the plane landed and they were deplaning, David helped her remove her carry-on from the overhead storage compartment. They gave each other polite good-byes, and Sydney walked off the plane ahead of him. As she was walking to the passenger pickup area, she pulled her phone out of her pocket to call Kennedy. A piece of paper fell out of her pocket. On it was written "DAVID KNOX—#555-365-0217."

Kennedy was waiting in the pickup lane for her. Sydney smiled to herself as she dragged her carry-on luggage all the way to the car.

She jumped into Kennedy's warm car. "You'll never guess what happened!"

"What?" said Kennedy.

"A guy I sat next to on the plane slipped his number into my pocket—without me realizing it!"

"Umm...that's romantic. What about Trey? You know...that guy you live with?"

"Oh, I'm not going to do anything about it. I just thought it was funny!" said Sydney.

"That was very smooth of him," said Kennedy.

"Yes, he was sooo good looking! It's always nice to be hit on by beautiful people. It's a confidence booster for sure!" said Sydney. "You know what? You should take his number, and you should call him!"

"What? That's weird. No, Syd. That's crazy. He gave his number to *you*."

"Just pretend that you're me, and then when you meet in person, you can surprise him!" Sydney laughed. "I doubt he'll be disappointed by a young, cute dentist."

"Well, this is the Year of Yes," said Kennedy.

EVERYONE LOVES BACON

Friday night of the first weekend in February, Kennedy went out in Hillcrest with her new friend, Robyn. Robyn and Kennedy had met through mutual friends in Little Rock at a young professionals' event. Robyn, a former news anchor, was a tall brunette whose makeup and clothing were always on point. She was now a spokeswoman for the department of health and human service. Although she was dating a guy who lived in Dallas, she had promised Kennedy that she would be her wingman for a night out in the Hillcrest neighborhood. They ended their night at one of the smokiest billiard rooms in Little Rock.

"There is always a ten-to-one guys-to-girls ratio at the Fountain," Robyn had said when she was convincing Kennedy that the smoky bar would be worth the risk.

One man at the Fountain in particular caught Kennedy's attention. His name was Kevin. He was tall, late twenties with curly long blond hair and blue eyes. He was playing pool when Kennedy accidentally bumped into him. Kevin told her that he was in real estate in Little Rock. She also found out that he was a patient of another doctor who worked in her clinic. She then tried to recruit him to be her next patient.

Kennedy and Kevin flirted back and forth for the next few hours. She enjoyed his easy conversation style and he seemed interested in her ideas on how to build the dentist practice where she worked.

It was one thirty in the morning, and Robyn was ready to go home, she interrupted the conversation and introduced herself to Kevin.

"Hi, I'm Kennedy's friend Robyn Smith. What's your name?"

"I'm Kevin...Kevin Bacon," he replied.

"Wait. Your name is Kevin Bacon?" said Kennedy. "No way."

"It's very true and unfortunate. However, my dance moves are not comparable," said Kevin Bacon.

Robyn was still getting antsy. She told Kennedy that she was ready to leave the bar. It was getting late.

Kennedy went with her without a fight. They took a couple of steps outside the bar.

"Kevin Bacon was so cute and tall!" said Kennedy.

"He definitely was," said Robyn. "Did he ask for your number?"

"No, he didn't at all."

"I have failed as a wing woman. I'll be right back."

Robyn turned around and went back into the bar. She came back out moments later.

"He now has your number!" she announced, waving her arms in the air and bowing to a pretend audience.

"Success! You're the best wing woman a girl could ask for!" yelled Kennedy. "We should probably go home now. I'm too old and drunk to stay up this late. Also, I need to wash the smell of smoke out of my hair."

"You're too uptight," said Robyn.

Kennedy spent the following night at home alone with Rosie. She was secretly hoping that Kevin Bacon would call and ask her on a date. One of the things Kennedy hated most about dating was waiting for men to call or text. There was no call. She had no such luck. Around one in the morning, Kennedy received a text message from Kevin.

All it said was "Hey, what's up?"

Kennedy didn't read the message until the next morning. She knew it was a booty text. He had seemed so nice. She had had such high hopes for him. She was really disappointed by this.

The following Saturday, she and Robyn went out to the bars again. This time, they went downtown to the Rev Room and Cache. Kennedy received another late-night text from Kevin.

Kevin at11:30 p.m.: Hey, what are you up to?

Kennedy at 11:45 p.m.: At Cache. You?

Kevin at 12:00 a.m.: I just saw you at Cache. I'm leaving soon. Come home with me.

Kennedy at 12:15 a.m.: Too late.

Kennedy had temporarily forgotten about the Year of Yes. Her feelings were hurt by his late-night texting. She thought that they had had good conversation and a lot in common. Kennedy realized at this moment that the Year of Yes might mean she would have to sacrifice her own moral code. Kennedy had never had a one-night stand.

The next Saturday, Kennedy went to visit her brother and sister in law in Dallas. They went out and bar-hopped that night in downtown. Kennedy thought this would be the perfect time to drunk prank Kevin.

Kennedy at 12:00 a.m.: Hey, what are you up to?

Kevin at 12:15 a.m.: I'm at Ciao Baci.

Kennedy at 12:16 a.m.: I'm at the Fountain. You should come here.

Kevin at 12:20 a.m.: If I come there, will you come home with me?

Kennedy at 12:25 a.m.: Yes.

Kevin at 12:40 a.m.: You still at the Fountain? I don't see you.

Kennedy at 12:50 a.m.: I'm in the back, by the bar.

Kevin at 1:00 a.m.: I still don't see you. Come home with me.

Kennedy at 1:45 a.m.: I'm not coming home with you. I'm not at the Fountain. I'm out of town. I thought we had a nice conversation when we met. Maybe you would ask me to go on a date or something.

Kevin at 1:50: Come home with me.

Kennedy: I don't do one-night stands. Also, you need to have more respect for women in general.

Kevin at 2:30 a.m.: Oh.

When Kennedy got back to the clinic the following Monday, she decided to look him up in the patient database. She was shocked to find out that he lived a street over from her. In fact, she ran by Kevin's house every day with Rosie. The marital status on his chart was also marked *M* for married. She was more shocked that he wanted her to come home with him if he was married. Either way, she was glad she had dodged that bullet.

A year and a half later, Kevin showed up in her chair as a new patient. Kennedy pretended that she did not remember him. At his exam, he was wearing a light-blue shirt that had picture of a single strip of bacon in the middle. The words around it read "Everyone Loves Bacon."

With his mouth clamped wide open, Kennedy politely reintroduced herself as Dr. James. When he was able to move his mouth again, Kevin kindly refreshed her memory of who he was. Kennedy made a mental note to no longer play pranks on men. They may become your patients.

3. MARCH

And the riverbank talks
Of the waters of March.
It's the promise of life;
It's the joy in your heart.

—Sofia

INTERNATIONAL
WOMEN'S DAY

The first weekend in March, Kennedy took Friday off and repaid a visit to Bailey in Atlanta. Kennedy stayed with Bailey in her new apartment in Buckhead. Their friends from dental school, Maureen and Jeff, also flew in for a continuing education conference. The group was wined and dined at a bar by one of the dental equipment supply companies at the conference. Then they went out in the Highlands with more friends from school as well as Bailey's boyfriend, Aaron.

The group of young dentists was at the Dark Horse Tavern when they ran into Sean, Bailey's ex-boyfriend.

He was there with his new girlfriend. Kennedy knew this situation was going to make Bailey uncomfortable.

"Let's talk about how Sean has lost all of his hair," said Kennedy, trying to distract her.

"He was balding, and he decided to shave his entire head," said Bailey. "I am so glad Aaron has a full head of hair."

Sean and Bailey's relationship had been a tumultuous one. They dated on and off for almost four years. Bailey and Sean were both career focused and driven. Their main issues revolved around him being Jewish and her Protestant. They both had loved each other but both had very dominant personalities. They tried but could not compromise on religion. That, along with the intensity of the professional competitiveness between them, led to the end of their relationship.

Kennedy felt compelled to say hi to Sean. She hadn't seen him in almost a year. He had been Sam's best friend in school. Regardless of who wasn't dating whom anymore, they had all been friends. Plus, she had had just enough to drink to feel like this meeting would go okay.

"Hi, Sean. How are you?" Kennedy said.

"Kennedy! I didn't expect to see you here. This is my girlfriend, Amanda," said Sean.

Kennedy shook Amanda's hand. Amanda was thin as a reed with wavy strawberry blonde hair hanging almost to her waist, pale skin and slightly slanted dark blue eyes. *She looks like a fairy*, thought Kennedy. From their brief exchange, Kennedy learned that Amanda was in her first year of pharmacy school in Atlanta. She had been a patient of Sean's, and that was how they had met.

"So, have you talked to Sam at all since you left him?" asked Sean.

"He mailed me a few of my things when I first moved to Little Rock. Which was nice of him. But I haven't talked to him since then," replied Kennedy.

"He's a really great guy. I never saw you two breaking up. I always thought that you two had this deep connection with each other," said Sean.

"We did have a deep connection. But, people change. He changed, and he wanted me to give up who I was so I could fit into his plan." Kennedy blurted out, as though she had just come to this realization.

"That's a shame. I hope you don't regret your decision. It was your loss," said Sean.

"My loss?" replied Kennedy "It's hard to think that not marrying a man because he is sexist is anyone's loss." she frowned and took a step back from Amanda and Sean.

"Sam is a great guy," Sean said. "That wasn't nice. Bailey is coming over here. Amanda and Bailey don't get along—we're out." Sean led Amanda out the door of the Dark Horse.

The pair left Kennedy standing there stunned.

"What did he say to you?" asked Bailey.

"Basically that I was an idiot for leaving Sam and that it was my loss," said Kennedy.

"That's not true at all," said Bailey. "It was Sam's loss. Not yours. We're both better off without those guys. Didn't you ever see that Lifetime movie about the two dentists that married each other and started a practice together? The guy dentist left his wife for a younger, newer version of his wife. Then she went crazy and killed him by driving over him with their SUV."

"I'm not sure I saw that one. But I'm glad we both didn't go there," said Kennedy, and she chugged the rest of her whiskey and Sprite.

Toward the end of the night, Kennedy walked up to the bar to order a drink. A tall man with startling dimples sidled up to the bar next to her. Between those incredible dimples were a perfect set of teeth, even and shining in the yellow pool of light from the bar.

"Hi, I'm Ben. What's your name?" said the stranger.

"I'm Kennedy. Nice to meet you."

"Do you live around this area?"

"No, I live in Arkansas. I'm just here for a conference," replied Kennedy.

"Arkansas? That's a long way away. What kind of conference?"

"A dental conference. I'm a dentist. Do you see that group of people over there? They're all dentists as well," said Kennedy, pointing to her friends at the door. They were all watching her flirt with Ben.

"You're a dentist? No wonder you have such pretty eyes," said Ben, smiling.

Kennedy laughed loudly at this comment.

"What?"

"Dentists are teeth—not eyes. When was the last time you had your teeth cleaned?"

"Well, that's embarrassing. I don't even remember. But, I do floss and brush my teeth every day."

"I can tell," smiled Kennedy.

Ben bought Kennedy two more drinks. They talked and hung out with some of her dental school friends.

Yes to a one-night stand…almost. Kennedy was intoxicated when Ben asked her to go home with him. She had determined that even if this guy was dumb, he was cute, and she was drunk enough to feel comfortable going back to his place. Kennedy got in the Uber with Ben, and they headed toward his house in North Highlands. They were kissing intensely in the car when Kennedy's phone started ringing. It was Bailey. She had called three times before Kennedy picked up.

"Where are you?" yelled Bailey over the music at the bar.

"I'm in the car with that Ben guy I met at the bar," said Kennedy.

"What? That guy with the Red Sox hat on?" said Bailey.

"That's the guy!" said Kennedy.

"Kennedy, you are not going home with that guy. This is so unsafe!" said Bailey.

"I'll be fine. I'm responsible," said Kennedy.

"Kennedy! Have the driver turn you back around!" yelled Bailey over the phone.

By this time, the Uber car was pulling up to Ben's house. Kennedy looked at Ben and made a sad face.

"I'm sorry. I'm going back to the bar to meet my friends," said Kennedy.

"What? I thought this was a sure thing!" said Ben.

"Will you take me back to the bar?" Kennedy asked the Uber driver.

"I sure will, honey!" said the driver.

"You're a tease," said Ben as he exited the car and slammed the door behind him.

The driver was named Angelica. Kennedy and she had a good conversation all the way back to the bar.

"You know that if I were a male driver, I probably wouldn't have turned the car around?" said Angelica.

"I know. I realized that. Again, thank you sooo much, Angelica!" said Kennedy.

"Yes, ma'am! Happy International Women's Day! I'll put the ride on his tab."

"Thanks, girl," said Kennedy as she rolled out of the cab in front of the bar.

MOUSTACHE MARCH

Yes, to meeting a stranger. Kennedy had made plans to meet up with a guy named David. David, the one who had met Sydney on the plane coming from Denver to Little Rock. Kennedy had been text-messaging back and forth with him for the last week. They had arranged to meet at Dugan's Irish Pub on Saint Patrick's Day. Kennedy did not realize at the time that this would be the busiest pub in Little Rock on Saint Patrick's Day.

She met up with Sarah and Drew, a couple of her friends that went to University of Arkansas with her. They all went to another bar before she was to head to Dugan's. None of them wanted to go to Dugan's after hearing how crowded it was. Kennedy had a couple of drinks there. Then she got the overwhelming feeling that she shouldn't go to Dugan's alone.

So she decided that she would just ditch David and meet him another time. He didn't know her. Technically, he still thought that she was Sydney. Kennedy and Sydney had Facebook stalked his photos. So, she knew what he looked like. Over six feet tall, light brown hair, large brown, kind eyes.

David had been texting her from Dugan's.

David: It's crazy busy at this bar…are you here yet?

Kennedy: No, having drinks with friends. I'm not going to make it to Dugan's.

After having a couple of drinks at Stone's Throw Brewery, Kennedy and her friends walked to Sticky Fingers a couple of blocks away to meet three more friends. People were out all over, wearing green and drinking green beer for Saint Patrick's Day.

The group sat down at a table for six. Most of these friends were people she had hung out with in college, and she had known Sarah and Drew for almost her entire life. Kennedy was having an amazing time catching up, laughing, and drinking in their company.

She had only been at Sticky Fingers for 15 minutes when Kennedy spotted a vaguely familiar face in the restaurant at the next table. It was David. *How funny that he would be at the same restaurant,* she thought. She wasn't sure whether she should go over and say hi or not. After all, he was practically a complete stranger.

Kennedy watched him for a while to see what he was doing. He was seated at the table with two other men. He looked exactly like his photo. He was a tall brunet and had broad shoulders and glasses that complemented his face. And those big brown eyes. One thing was different from his photo: he had a thin mustache growing on his upper lip. *That's a deal breaker*, she thought.

She watched him pick up his phone and type something. A few seconds later, her iPhone vibrated. It was a text message from David.

David: We decided to go to Sticky Fingers.

Kennedy knew this already. She didn't want to tell him she was staring right at him while he was texting her. So she recruited her friend, Sarah, to go with her to approach the table of the three men with her.

Be bold, she thought. *This is the Year of Yes.*

Kennedy and Sarah walked up to the table with the three men.

"Are you David Knox?" asked Kennedy.

"My friends call me Dave, yes. That's me. Who are you?"

"I'm Kennedy James. I'm friends with Sydney. I'm the one you've been texting. I told you I was going to be at Dugan's. Then I decided not to go," said Kennedy.

"So you bailed on me, and you're not even Sydney? This is a little confusing," said David, astonished.

"Sydney has a boyfriend and lives in Denver. So she gave you my number instead. I hope you're not too disappointed," she said. *Be bold*, she thought.

"Well, Kennedy, it's nice to meet you. This is my little brother, Thomas, and my flying buddy, Will. We're celebrating Thomas's twenty-first birthday tonight. Also, Will leaves for Japan next week. Would you like to take a seat?" asked David.

Kennedy pulled up a chair. She could tell that Sarah was getting uncomfortable sitting at the table full of strange men. She whispered to her that she would be okay there by herself, and Sarah went back to their previous table.

"Do you live here in Little Rock?" asked Dave.

"Yes, I moved here in January," said Kennedy.

"Me too. I was stationed in Japan before this. Where did you move from?"

"North Carolina."

"What do you do, Kennedy, for a living? Are you from North Carolina originally?" asked David.

"No, I'm from northwest Arkansas. I'm a dentist here now. I went to college at U of A in Fayetteville and I graduated from the University of Missouri Dental School in May. I followed a guy after that and moved to North Carolina with him."

"I'm guessing you two are no longer together?"

"Your guess is correct," said Kennedy, blushing a little.

Then the conversation turned to David's brother, Thomas. He somehow threw the conversation into a downward spiral with one simple question. "What church do you go to here in town?" Thomas asked Kennedy.

Kennedy had to think about the answer to this. *When was the last time I went to church?*

"I don't go that often, but when I do, I go to Holy Souls in Hillcrest."

"So you're Catholic?" said Thomas.

"Yes," said Kennedy.

"We're Catholic also," said Thomas. "We go to Saint Andrew's downtown. Do you lean toward more conservative or more liberal?"

Wow, that's a little invasive, thought Kennedy. She had been taught not to talk about three things when she first met people: religion, money, and politics. She knew what they were doing, though. His brother was helping David find deal breakers. David most likely had a checklist in his head of what he wanted in a woman. A checklist of deal breakers is necessary when seeking a significant other. Kennedy had failed to have one in her last relationship. However, she had just met this man. She did not owe him anything.

"I lean more liberal than conservative. My mother is a Democrat, and my father is a Republican. I'm also a Democrat, if you really want to know how I'm registered to vote."

"We're Republican," replied Thomas. "What are your thoughts on abortion?"

Not happening, thought Kennedy.

Just as they were about to delve into a political issue that was beyond the realm of Sticky Fingers, Sarah came back to the table to tell Kennedy they were leaving. Sarah asked if Kennedy needed a ride. Kennedy quickly said yes.

"Looks like my ride is leaving. It was nice to meet all of you," said Kennedy. She got up and walked out with the rest of the group she had come with, thanking herself for not meeting up with him alone.

"What did you think of David?" Sarah asked. "He's extremely attractive!"

"He's way too political for me," said Kennedy. "Also, his brother asked me where I stood on abortion! He was way too intense for me."

Sarah laughed. "Well, at least you met him. Now, on to the next guy! Do you remember Drew's friend Steve? He thinks you're cute. We're meeting him at the piano bar two blocks away."

"I thought you said we were going home," said Kennedy.

"That was just a tactic to see if you wanted to leave," said Sarah.

"Thank you for that! It really was perfect timing!"

Kennedy spent the rest of the night drinking and having a fun time with Steve, Drew, and Sarah. She wrote the handsome brown-eyed David off as a loss. Steve was cute and well educated and had a steady engineering job. At the age of twenty-five, he was two years younger than she was. But more importantly he didn't ask any in-depth questions about her life.

The four discovered the dance club downstairs from Willy D's piano bar. When they walked in, Steve was still wearing his green Saint Patrick's Day sunglasses, and the lenses of the sunglasses were in the shape of beer mugs. The four immediately started dancing.

There were very few people on the dance floor. Steve was more of a comedic dancer. In other words, he was not afraid to break it down on the dance floor. Not too long after they started dancing, a large bouncer stationed next to the DJ walked over to Steve and said something in his ear. Steve then removed his green, beer-mug-shaped sunglasses.

"Sunglasses aren't allowed inside here!" he yelled over the music in Kennedy's ear.

"Why not?" Kennedy yelled back.

"It's dress code. Too many thugs...too little time!" yelled Steve, smiling.

"That's ridiculous!" yelled Kennedy. Then she took the sunglasses off of Steve's head and put them over her eyes. She started dancing uncontrollably.

The same large, very buff bouncer walked back over to the group. This time, he took Steve to the side and talked to him again, right in his ear. He was pointing right at Kennedy.

"What did he say?" Kennedy asked Steve.

"He said that if my girlfriend doesn't take those sunglasses off, he'll kick my ass!" Steve yelled.

Kennedy laughed and kept dancing.

Steve was starting to look concerned. "You should probably take those off."

"I'm not your girlfriend! You're not responsible for me! We literally just met! This is bullshit! I'm not taking these off! That bouncer should have asked me himself to take them off. I'm going to go tell him that!" yelled Kennedy.

As she started walking toward the bouncer, Steve grabbed her arm and pulled her to the stairs. "That is one large dude, and I do not want to get my ass kicked tonight," he said.

"This is ridiculous. I'm responsible for myself!" said Kennedy. "And now I'm hungry. Let's get some food."

They met up with Sarah and Drew and walked to a late-night diner. While they were eating, Kennedy apologized to Steve for putting his life in danger. Then they walked to Sarah and Drew's place.

Kennedy slept in the twin guest bed, and Steve slept on the couch. The next day he didn't ask for her number. Kennedy decided that she had probably been slightly obnoxious last night. But she still thought the bouncer's ban on sunglasses was ridiculous.

The Wednesday after the Saint Patrick's Day weekend, Kennedy got a call from David, the pilot, while she was at work. He left a voice message asking her if she wanted to meet for drinks. She thought it was strange that he had called and left a voice message instead of texting her. It was oddly refreshing.

If it weren't the Year of Yes, I would not say yes to drinks with him, Kennedy told herself.

TINDER NIGHTMARE

"I didn't know whether I should tell you or not. But I've known you and Drew for ten years now. I met you both at the beginning of your relationship. I've been there through some of your ups and down. For both of you. I feel like I am equally both of your friends," Kennedy told Sarah. They were sitting at the dog park watching their dogs fight over a ball.

"Kennedy, just tell me what it is!" cried Sarah.

"I don't want this to ruin our friendship. But I thought over and over again, would I want to know? The answer is, yes, I would want to know," said Kennedy.

"What is it?" Sarah asked.

Kennedy took a deep breath and said, "Okay, I found Drew on Tinder when you were in Boston last week."

"What!" cried Sarah.

"I took a screenshot to show you," said Kennedy.

"No...no, I don't want to see it. I believe you. I don't want to. But I do. What do I do now?" asked Sarah.

"I've never been in this situation before. But, if it were me, I would ask him why he was on it. Then, if he didn't give a reasonable explanation, I would break up with him."

"That sounds rational," said Sarah. Kennedy could see tears running down Sarah's cheeks from underneath her sunglasses.

"What's dating like in Little Rock?" Sarah asked.

"Constant disappointment."

ROMANTIC FEMINIST

Kennedy met David on the following Thursday at an Irish pub in midtown. It was seven in the evening, and the bar was practically empty. When she walked in, David was having a lively conversation with the bartender. They were discussing the news story on the bar television about the Malaysian aircraft that had gone missing.

"You know they just find random pilots to interview for these things. That man is probably a private small-plane pilot who has no idea how to fly a commercial plane or what actually could have happened to that Malaysian airliner," David was telling the bartender.

"Do you know what actually happened to the Malaysian airliner?" Kennedy asked from behind David.

He turned around on his stool to face Kennedy. "No, but I have a few good theories. One of them might involve Russia."

He stood up and gave her a hug. He was very tall and broad shouldered. Kennedy typically dated shorter men. She always attributed this quirky choice to her dominant personality. Kennedy again noticed how easy it was to get lost in his large dark brown eyes but she was disappointed to note that he was still sporting that thin, caterpillar-like moustache. *Just can't do it,* she thought.

Kennedy ordered a Stella Artois and the two started in on first date banter. She felt the conversation was flowing easily. Then, she decided to bring up what had happened on their first meet and greet. "Your brother seems pretty intense about his religion and politics. What's that all about?" she asked.

"Thomas can be very forward. He is very young and passionate in his convictions. He told me he didn't like you because you were a feminist."

"And yet, you still asked me out for drinks?" asked Kennedy

"I am not my brother," said David.

"I will take that answer. However, I don't think wanting equality for men and women is a bad thing," said Kennedy

"The first time I met you, you said that you lean more toward the liberal side of things. You seem well educated, independent, yet you seem to have something against men. That tells me you're a feminist. You walk around like you don't need a man if you don't want one. You obviously could get one because you're a very pretty and intelligent women. Thomas just happens to hate feminists," said David.

"Wow! You're a little like Thomas, jumping right in and telling me I walk around like I don't need a man or have something against them. Maybe there is something wrong with Thomas for thinking that. Maybe it's just the years and years of brainwashing that he's been subjected to about how all women are delicate flowers to be put on a pedestal and protected. We're all taught that, right?" Kennedy said only half-teasing.

"The thing about you is, you don't seem concerned about the fact that you're single," said David.

"I don't have to be concerned. My family is concerned enough for me," said Kennedy, getting frustrated with Captain Dave. But also attracted to him and weirdly excited to be arguing with him.

"Are you going to work when you have children?"

"I can't imagine myself not working when I have children. I don't have a problem with women who want to stay at home, though. Sometimes I wish I could stay at home more with my puppy to take care of her. I understand a woman's urge to want to stay home and nurture her children. Especially when they are young. But there's nothing like a good education to fall back on," said Kennedy.

"Also, there is this huge stigma to being a feminist. It's like you, as men, are trained to think that every woman who is a feminist is a lesbian who walks around acting butch and busting men's balls. I have nothing against lesbians, and I think everyone should be exactly what they want to be in life. Unless that person wants to be a murderer or something. Anyways, I'm a straight, hardworking female who just happens to be a romantic and a feminist."

"You can't be a romantic feminist. That's just too conflicting," said David.

"I don't think so. Why can't I have it all? Why can't I have a great career, a family, and a husband who supports my choices and works just as hard as I do? Sheryl Sandberg does it. Why can't I also be paid as much as a male dentist who has the same education and experience? I shouldn't be still asking these questions." she said.

"I have no idea who Sheryl Sandberg is. But I will agree with you that women and men should get paid equally. Also, my mother is a high-school principal who works very hard and supports our family along with my father."

"Equal pay is the basic tenet of feminism. So technically you're a feminist. But, you still talk about it with disdain." asked Kennedy.

"I think women become men haters. We, as men, need to feel needed and substantial," said David.

"I think that could be said for everyone—not just men. We, as humans, need to feel needed and substantial. That's just a selfish excuse."

"Regardless, I hate the theory that everything bad in the world stems from white male oppression. Furthermore, that women think that men give no respect and hold no responsibility to the preciousness of human life, which women have a special role in creating. If you believe this, then you will never be able to be happy with a man," said David. Then he took a swig of his beer.

"Let's just say I've been jaded. It's not all men. You don't know what I deal with every day at work, with patients and colleagues," said Kennedy. Kennedy was getting frustrated with this conversation.

They had been debating for an hour when a man walked up onto the small stage and announced that Wednesday night was karaoke night at Hibernia. They looked around and realized that the bar had filled with people while they had been talking in their own little world.

Kennedy and David took turns singing. They weren't afraid to embarrass themselves at this dive bar. David sang a song by Frank Sinatra. Several people in the bar clapped for him. Kennedy got up and sang the new song by Lorde, "Royals." She was more comfortable singing on this tiny stage. There was a large group of women in the back of the bar who started yelling and clapping for her during the song.

"I've never heard that song before," said David. "I don't listen to a lot of hip-hop."

"Technically, I think that song is played on the pop radio stations. I don't listen to hip-hop much either. Do you listen to the radio?" asked Kennedy, again teasing him.

"The only radio station my Land Cruiser gets is National Public Radio," said David.

"I love NPR," said Kennedy.

"You would," replied David with a smirk.

Kennedy's 10:00 p.m. alarm went off on her phone to remind her to take her birth control. It was also time to go. They had been at this bar for four hours. Three more hours than Kennedy had expected.

The alarm prompted David to say that it was time to go as well. Somehow, they had lost track of time. He was supposed to have a Skype date with his ex-girlfriend from Colorado that night at 9:00 p.m. This had not happened.

David walked Kennedy to her car. He told her how much fun he had had with her that night. He put his hand on the small of her back and drew her in for a kiss. It was an easy kiss. To Kennedy, it felt effortless.

Kennedy's phone rang as she was driving home. It was Sydney.

"How'd your date go?" asked Sydney.

"It was okay…kind of strange," said Kennedy.

"Just okay? This is the pilot guy that I met on the plane, right?"

"Yes, it was."

"Why was it so strange?"

"It was strange because we debated for an hour of the date. Then we sang karaoke. Then he kissed me. And it was an awesome kiss. I'm confused. Also, he still has that horrendous moustache. I just can't stand that moustache!" said Kennedy.

"Do you think you'd go out with him again?"

"Yes…for some odd reason, I think that I would."

SKINNY LOVE

David did ask her out on another date. This time it was on Friday night. He told her that he was going to surprise her.

"I hope it's tickets to see *Les Miserables*," Kennedy had told him.

"How did you know? That's exactly what the surprise was," David had said over the phone.

He sent her a text message during the day on Friday saying that the show had been sold out. He had been unable to get tickets. He told her that he would take her somewhere else that was just as exciting.

Kennedy was disappointed. She had gotten her hopes up about seeing *Les Miserables*. She had been wanting someone to go with her since the play had come to town. It was her favorite musical of all time.

Kennedy had a busy day at work. Then she rushed home to get ready to go out. David was going to be there at seven. She went on a run with Rosie and then showered. He had told her to dress fancy. So she put on a body-hugging Calvin Klein dress and started searching for a pair of heels. Kennedy typically did not wear high heels. She was a flat-shoe-wearing kind of girl. But for the first time in a long time, she had a date with a taller man. *Yes, to high heels.*

David showed up at her doorstep ten minutes early. She was not completely ready. Mainly, she just couldn't find the high heels that she had her mind set on wearing. David stood in her foyer and played with Rosie while Kennedy scrambled to find her shoes.

"You'd look beautiful even if you were to go barefoot," said David.

What a line, thought Kennedy.

After twenty more minutes, Kennedy was ready to go, and Rosie was safe and sound in her kennel. Kennedy had never seen David's car before. It was a Land Cruiser that he had imported from Japan. The driver's seat was on the right-hand side instead of the left. Kennedy did not realize this. David had gone around to the passenger side, which was the left side, to open the car door for her. Kennedy had gone to the right side—what should have been the passenger side—to open her own door.

They both opened the doors at the same time. They looked at each other and laughed.

"I didn't know you drove on the wrong side," said Kennedy.

"This is the right side for me," said David.

Kennedy walked around the car and let David help her into the elevated seats. She had never ridden in a car with the steering wheel on the other side. It was a new adventure for her.

David would not tell Kennedy where he was taking her. However, the car was headed toward downtown. Kennedy thought they were going to the Capitol Hotel for a nice dinner. She would feel silly being dressed up in Little Rock for nothing less. Instead, David pulled his car into the parking lot across the street from the Repertory Theatre. It was then that it dawned on Kennedy: they were going to see *Les Miserables*! He had tricked her into thinking that he couldn't get tickets so that it would still be a surprise.

In the entrance of the theater, Kennedy and David ran into one of the dentists in Kennedy's office. Dr. Sims said hello to both of them. Kennedy introduced David to Dr. Sims, and Dr. Sims introduced them to his wife.

"I've heard you're going to give my husband a run for his money in patient care," said Mrs. Sims.

"And I heard that Dr. Sims was voted the best dentist in Little Rock by the *Arkansas Gazette.* That's going to be a hard one to beat!" replied Kennedy.

"We'll see you two later. It was nice to meet both of you," said Dr. Sims as he escorted his wife into the theater.

Kennedy was starving. Having assumed that the surprise would be dinner, she hadn't eaten beforehand. She suggested they get food from the concession upstairs before the show.

Kennedy grabbed a turkey sandwich wrapped in cellophane, and David picked out a tuna sandwich. They both ordered beers off the menu.

When they sat down to eat, David stared at Kennedy with a confused expression while she ate.

"Is there something wrong?" asked Kennedy in between bites.

"No, it's just that you're eating a turkey sandwich."

"Yes, and?"

"It's Friday, during Lent."

"Oh my gosh—I didn't even realize today was Friday!" said Kennedy. "I was so hungry! You know, you were the one who bought me this, right? Didn't this occur to you when you were buying it?"

"It did, but I wasn't going to stop you from eating it."

"Well, I guess it's time to tell you that I'm not a very devout Catholic," said Kennedy.

"You're in your twenties. I understand. We all have our lapses in our faith."

"What happened to your mustache?" asked Kennedy, glad that it was gone.

"I shaved it off. I couldn't handle it anymore. It was for Mustache March."

"I've heard of No-Shave November and Movember, but Mustache March is a new one."

"It's a pilot thing. Besides, I saw you staring at it on our last date. I have a feeling you don't like mustaches." David chuckled.

"You're right; I hate mustaches. Sorry. I'm really not sorry." Kennedy laughed.

They were done eating just as the lights flickered, indicating they needed to go into the theater. David grabbed her hand, and they held hands walking in. Kennedy felt as if she were a teenager again.

When they found their seats, they just happened to be right next to Dr. and Mrs. Sims. David put his arm around her the entire date. Kennedy felt awkward sitting next to a colleague while on a date. The Sims did not seem to mind too much. Kennedy and David enjoyed the show tremendously. They both knew most of the lyrics. Kennedy tried her hardest not to sing out loud.

After the show, David suggested they go for drinks somewhere. He took her to his favorite place in Hillcrest, called SO. It was a small, private restaurant that Kennedy had no idea existed. It had a fancy, big-city vibe that Kennedy loved. It was eleven o'clock when they arrived, and there were only a few people in the restaurant. Kennedy and David sat at the bar. Kennedy ordered an Irish coffee because she was exhausted, and David ordered a bottle of red wine for both of them.

That night, Kennedy learned David was leaving at the end of June. Air force pilots came in and out of

Little Rock for training, and he was constantly moving. This time he was being reassigned to Albuquerque, New Mexico. Kennedy was a little disappointed but decided to be okay with this. She was not prepared for a serious relationship at this particular moment.

The two stayed at SO until the bar closed around two thirty in the morning. The song "Skinny Love," sung by Birdie, came on in the restaurant. Kennedy realized that that was what their relationship might be. The time was swept away from them. David drove Kennedy back to her townhouse. Then he stayed the night at her place, as he would every other night for the next couple of weeks.

Come on, skinny love, just last the year,
Pour a little salt; we were never here…

─<|+ +|>─

Kennedy: Do you want me to tell you something disgusting?
David: Yes, please.
Kennedy: I found out why Rosie was sick.
David: Why?
Kennedy: She threw up on the back porch. There was a townhousem in it.
David: Oh, gross! That might have been my fault. I'm so sorry. I threw it on the floor.
Kennedy: It's okay. Just please don't do it again. I really don't want to have to pay for a surgery

because a townhousem is wrapped around my puppy's intestines. You haven't had a puppy before. Keep in mind that everything on the floor is fair game.
David: 10-4. :-). Yes, ma'am.

4. APRIL

April, come she will
When streams are ripe and swelled with rain.

—Simon and Garfunkel

STRANGER DANGER

The first weekend in April, Kennedy's friend Adrian, who lived in Florida, asked Kennedy if she wanted to be flown to Jacksonville for a dental conference. Adrian was three years old than Kennedy in school. Kennedy and Adrian had gone on a dental mission trip together to Honduras and became fast friends. Adrian was thin, spunky, and outgoing with wild brown curly hair. The trip would be paid for by one of the companies hosting the conference. Of course, Kennedy said yes.

David had kindly offered to keep Rosie while she was out of town. At this point David and Kennedy had spent almost every day together since their date to see *Les Miserables*. Also, the only other option she had was to board Rosie for the weekend. So she took him up on the offer.

Kennedy flew out on a Thursday morning. Her first connection was from Little Rock to Atlanta. When the plane landed in Atlanta, she turned the Wi-Fi on her iPhone back on. She had a Snapchat from a name that she did not know.

She opened the Snapchat, and it was a picture of a plane ticket. The ticket number was circled, and there was a message that said, "Are you on this flight?"

Kennedy's stomach started turning. Yes, she was on that flight! She started looking around for someone she knew. She did not recognize any of the people around her. Who was this person, and how did he or she know her? Was she being stalked? Was this how she was going to die?

She put the hood of her coat on along with her sunglasses. She exited the plane in dramatic style, as quickly as possible, and started briskly walking to her next gate. She searched for any passengers she might recognize, but she did not see any. She was panicking.

When she sat down at her next gate, Kennedy started searching the Internet for that screen name. All she could come up with was a guy named Steven who lived in Detroit. There was no photo.

She sent a Snapchat back to the unknown Snapchatter. All the message said was, "Who is this?"

The unknown messenger failed to reply.

ELEVATORS AND
ALCOHOL

Kennedy arrived in Florida a little shaken by the strange Snapchat message but ready for the conference. She had her own hotel room. The last three years she had spent going to conferences as a student, she had shared a room with Sam. Kennedy she felt a rush of excitement from the independence that this trip brought.

She hadn't seen her friend Adrian since their mission trip in Honduras last May. The two were ecstatic to see each other. This wasn't exactly a conference. This was more of a promotional thing for one of the dental-drill producers. The company that was hosting the conference was wining and dining them until Saturday, when they had to fly back home.

On Friday, Kennedy and Adrian spent all day in class. Then they were treated to a full-course meal with all-you-can-drink wine. Kennedy still felt like a student at times. Most of the other doctors at the workshop were older than she was. Even Adrian had been two years ahead of her in school and was three years older. After all, she had only been out of dental school for almost a year.

"Where are you working now? Here in Jacksonville?" asked Kennedy.

"Well, yes. I'm doing fill-in work right now," said Adrian.

"Really? I thought you were working for a private practice."

"I was. This is embarrassing to say, but I was let go from the office where I was working," said Adrian.

"What? How does that even happen?"

"There were two established doctors in this practice. They hired me because an older doctor was retiring and cutting back on hours. So I started working at the office full time, and the older doctor cut back to part time. However, I was hardly getting patients in the door. Then I found out that they were only scheduling me with overflow patients that the other two doctors didn't want. They didn't do any advertising for me, and I was on a base-salary-plus-bonus model. I wasn't seeing enough patients to even reach my bonus. Finally, the doctor who was retiring decided he wanted to come back full time. So they fired me because they couldn't afford to pay me full time."

"That's ridiculous! They didn't even give you the opportunity to get new patients in the door. I know you're a good dentist. You're personable, you're residency trained, and Board Certified." said Kennedy.

"I know. I realize that. However, it's still a major blow to my ego. So this weekend I have to socialize with the dentists in this area to find out if anyone is hiring," said Adrian.

"I'm so sorry; I didn't realize. Are you getting along okay? Do you have many student loans?" said Kennedy. She realized how lucky she was to have a full-time job with nice benefits. She was still paying quite a bit each month on her student loans but had her parents to fall back on for help.

"Luckily, Mike is being really supportive and helping pay the bills. I don't know what I would do without my husband," said Adrian. "Speaking of that, how is the single life treating you?"

"It's going pretty well. I'm kind of seeing this air force pilot right now. But it's not too serious. Also, he's moving in two months. So I think he's just going to be my rebound man," said Kennedy.

"That's good. Everyone needs one of those after what you went through," said Adrian.

"Thanks, I guess. I'm sure other people have been through worse. At least it wasn't a divorce," said Kennedy.

"So, what was your breaking point?"

"What do you mean, 'breaking point'?"

"When you lived with Sam. I know you two were having problems. But there must have been a moment when you decided that you were completely done," said Adrian.

"Let me think. Actually, it was a really dumb breaking point. But I'll tell you anyways," said Kennedy.

"Spill away!" said Adrian.

"So one weekend last fall, we were hanging out with Sam's parents and his parents' friends. His parents took us out on their friends' boat on the coast of eastern North Carolina. We had been riding on the boat for an hour or so on an inlet in swampy water. At this point I realized I had to really go to the bathroom. This is too much information, but I was on my period, and I also really needed to change my tampon.

"Just when I thought we were headed back to the shore, the driver took a left turn, and we drove into the wide-open sound channel of the ocean with no docks in sight. So now we were nowhere near shore. We were fully dressed. It wasn't like I could jump into the water fully clothed to pee. I panicked a little, and I told Sam that I had to go the bathroom sooner rather than later.

Sam whispered to the driver that I needed to use the bathroom. The driver was a middle-aged man with a moustache and a fishing shirt on. He turned to me and laughed.

"'I heard you had to go to the bathroom! Number one or number two?' he yelled over the roaring engine. He laughed loudly at his joke. Everyone on the boat stared at me. This was just the beginning of the harassment that ensued. He kept heckling me about having to go to the bathroom. Like he was a twelve-year-old picking on a girl in his class. I was so uncomfortable, and my stomach hurt terribly. I have raging PMS and the last thing I needed was a grown man teasing me about having to go to the bathroom."

"Finally, I looked at him and said, 'Why don't you just stop talking?' I said it in a very abrupt and condescending tone. We did stop shortly after that on a public dock, and I was able to go to the bathroom. The other women in the boat said they had to go too. But they didn't want to say anything. I swear I would have punched him if I could."

"That guy sounds like a jerk!" said Adrian.

"That's not the worst part of the story. When I got back on the boat, Sam was furious with me. He told me that I had embarrassed him by being rude to his dad's friend. Sam said that the guy didn't think I liked him very much. He was right. I didn't like him at all. He'd tried to embarrass me and I'd just snapped at him.

There was nothing wrong with what I did. Anyways, the main reason this was a breaking point was because this was the moment I realized that Sam was never going to defend me. I was in his world, with no one on my side for the rest of my life. He would always put his friends' and family's thoughts and opinions in front of mine."

"You're right. You always want to marry someone who will defend you when you're being harassed. You should write a blog or a book about your breakup," said Adrian.

"Ha! Really? Would you read it? I mean, no one dies in the story, and no one cheats. It would just be about a seven-month breakup of an engagement."

"I can picture myself reading right now, on the beach, with a Lime-A-Rita in my hand." Adrian laughed.

"Thanks. I am in the Year of Yes. Maybe I'll start writing. I've heard it can be therapeutic," said Kennedy.

After dinner that night, Kennedy was getting a drink from the bar when she noticed the guy sitting three chairs to the left of her. She remembered that he had sat next to her and Adrian at their table at dinner. She had noticed that he did not talk much. His dark hair was combed back and his face carefully structured. He had a Roman nose and a thin pair of lips that was in a form of a smirk. He saw her at the bar too and moved closer to talk to her.

"I noticed that you were at my table at dinner. Where do you practice?" he asked her.

"I'm in Little Rock," said Kennedy.

"Little Rock?" he said. "What is there to do in Little Rock? I don't think I've met anyone from Arkansas, ever."

"That's why they call us the flyover state. There are plenty of things to do in Arkansas, like goin' cow teepin' and goin' to Wal-Mart," said Kennedy in her thickest drawl.

Then, in her usual Midwest accent, she said, "Where do you practice? California?"

"Close. Portland."

"Oh, I should have known by your paleness."

"My name is Collin Myers. Nice to meet you."

"I'm Kennedy James. Nice to meet you as well. Are you here by yourself?"

"Yes. What was your personality type on the test today?" asked Collin.

"I was a high I, for interactive. Apparently I feed off of social networking. What about you?"

"I was a high C. Conscientious. I'm concerned about getting things precise," said Collin.

"What was your worst flaw?"

"I spend so much time trying to do what is right that I tend to overlook what is best for patients in their certain situations. I'll agree to disagree on that one. I think the personality tests can just be a bunch of bullshit that is more often than not apt to change," said Collin. "What was yours?"

"My worst quality is that I'm lax when it comes to reprimanding my patients when they don't follow my directions. The personality test also told me that I have a tendency to flaunt my independence."

"Is it true?" asked Collin.

"It's true. Even more so lately. Maybe one day I won't flaunt it. But right now, I can't be held down," said Kennedy after taking a drink of her beer. "A couple of us are going out for drinks close to the hotel after this. Do you want to come?"

"Sure. Who all is going?" asked Collin.

"It will be those three women waiting for us by the door and you," said Kennedy.

"That works for me." He smiled.

The five young dentists spent the rest of the night barhopping around Jacksonville. Kennedy had a beer at every bar they hit. They all talked mainly about teeth, dental procedures, patient care, and dealing with staff issues. Any other person hanging out with them would have found this conversation to be incredibly banal. However, the group found comfort in being able to discuss their careers with fellow professionals.

Later in the night, Collin started talking to the women, his colleagues, about his children. Collin admitted that he was thirty years old and had two children. *It is normal to be thirty years old and have two or more children,* thought Kennedy. However, the older of his children was fifteen years old, and the younger was twelve. He told the women how strange it was to be this young and dealing with teenagers. He and his ex-wife were now dealing with issues that made them feel almost hypocritical, considering what they had done when they were teenagers.

When the night was over, the group stumbled back to the hotel. They were all intoxicated with food and booze. Collin and Kennedy were on the same floor. The other girls were on the first floor. They rode the elevator up to their floor together. Collin reached for Kennedy's hand and then began kissing her. He tasted like the smoky bourbon he had been drinking. Kennedy thought this was delicious. This was a heated elevator make-out session that Kennedy was not going to fight. At least for the moment.

But when the doors opened, she gave him one more kiss. She then pushed him away and said, "I'm sorry; I can't. Good night." Then she turned and walked toward her hotel room without looking back. Even in her inebriated state, she still had a certain air force pilot on her mind.

THE BOSS ON THE BUS

Kennedy's flight left at eight the next morning. When she boarded the shuttle to the airport, she found a seat next to Collin. The bus was full of older doctors they had met the last couple of days.

"I forgot to ask you something last night," said Collin.

Kennedy could feel the men around her perking up their ears.

"Was it how to properly extract a tooth without anesthesia and causing the patient pain?" said Kennedy sarcastically.

The men around her laughed. Collin then realized that they were all listening. "No, I was just wondering how much student-loan debt you had accrued so I could compare it to mine," he said. Kennedy could tell that this was not the question he really wanted to ask her.

"That's a reasonable question," said Kennedy. The men around her continued to listen as she talked about her student-loan debt.

Collin and Kennedy made it through the security line together with small talk. Before she left Collin to get on her flight, he pulled her aside and asked her not to tell anyone about their passionate elevator ride. He was actually still married. *Thank God I did not sleep with him,* thought Kennedy.

It was still only Saturday, and Kennedy had a four-hour layover to look forward to at the Atlanta airport. She thought about Bailey and wondered how she was doing. So she sent her a text hoping it was something fun. She didn't feel like going back to Little Rock just yet.

Kennedy: Hey, I'm in Atlanta on a four-hour layover. What are you up to?

Bailey: I'm going to see Bruce Springsteen in concert tonight with a bunch of people. You should stay in town!

Kennedy: That sounds like a lot of fun. I probably wouldn't be able to get concert tickets near you, though.

Bailey: We have general admission tickets in the grass. There are still some available online. You know you have to say yes!

Kennedy: Okay, let me check flight prices.

The price was a hundred dollars for Kennedy to fly back from Atlanta to Little Rock the next day. Her trip thus far had been free. So Kennedy decided to purchase the ticket and stay in Atlanta for the night.

She called David after she purchased the ticket and asked him to keep Rosie one more night. He said that he didn't mind at all. David told her that he and his brother had taken her to the farmer's market that morning. He said that they had gotten a lot of compliments on how cute their dog was.

"Rosie is a real lady magnet," said David.

"I'm going to pretend I didn't hear that. Thanks again for keeping her," said Kennedy.

Kennedy thought about the make-out session in the elevator she had with Collin the night before. She felt a twinge of guilt, as if she had cheated on David. Collin definitely had cheated on his wife. She was guessing that wasn't the first time. Kennedy knew she should not feel she had cheated on David. She wasn't used to being in this unknown dating area. Before this, Kennedy had been a serial monogamist. She and David had not defined the relationship. He had not asked her to be his girlfriend. On the other hand, she wouldn't want to know if he was making out with other girls while she was out of town and taking care of Rosie.

Thirty minutes later, Bailey picked Kennedy up from the airport. Kennedy had only brought business clothes for her trip. It was an unusually hot Saturday in April, and she did not want to wear slacks to an outdoor Bruce Springsteen concert. Bailey let Kennedy borrow one of her dresses. Unfortunately for Kennedy, Bailey was four inches shorter than she was, ten pounds lighter, and wore mainly petites. Kennedy found one dress in Bailey's closet that she could squeeze into semi comfortably. The dress made her 32 B-cup boobs look a lot larger than they actually were. They also made her butt look enormous. She felt pale and bloated. But this was another "yes" in the Year of Yes. There was no time for insecurities about her body to stop this adventure.

The girls loaded into an Uber that took them to Buckhead to meet Bailey's friends. They shared a three-bedroom penthouse suite in one of the high-end apartment complexes there. After making it through security and getting someone to fob them into the elevator, Kennedy and Bailey walked into a room of about twenty people. There were equal numbers of men and women, all in their mid-twenties. It was four in the afternoon, and the group had all been drinking since two. Bailey knew everyone in the room and introduced Kennedy to them. She told the story a few times of how Kennedy was on a layover and decided to stay in Atlanta for the night.

Kennedy was two beers in when someone in the room announced that the party bus had arrived. She had not been informed that they were taking a party bus. Everyone began loading up coolers full of drinks to enjoy onto the bus. Then the group headed downstairs to board the bus.

This bus was an old school bus that had been freshly painted bright orange. The windows were blacked out so that only the driver could see out of the windshield. The seats in the front were spaced like booth seating in a restaurant. In the back, there was a large open area with a shiny silver pole from the floor to the ceiling. There were seats on both sides facing the pole. The far back of the bus was a curtained area for the stripper to change or put her props. Yes, there was a hired stripper on this bus.

The group of around twenty or so millennials loaded their coolers into the bus and turned up the music loud. Bailey told Kennedy that they had rented out a party bus from this company before, and it had been a lot of fun. Kennedy was already tipsy at this point and was feeling a little claustrophobic.

Kennedy had been talking to a guy named Tyler back at the apartment, and he seemed to want to sit right next to her on the bus. He kept calling her Little Rock. Either he thought it was cute, or he was drunk and could not remember her name. Kennedy couldn't decide.

Kennedy and Bailey were drinking beer and playing a game of 'never have I ever' when the bus came to a dead stop on I-85 West. With the windows blacked out, it took about ten minutes for the group to realize that the bus wasn't moving and traffic around them was.

Kennedy squeezed her way through to the front of the bus to see the stripper sitting in the driver's seat and the bus driver opening the hood which was billowing smoke. Everyone on the bus slowly began to pick up on the fact that the bus was not going to be fixed. They were stuck in the third lane of a five-lane interstate in an old school bus, with all of the windows blacked out.

About twenty minutes later, Kennedy was starting to have a small panic attack. It was a humid afternoon and ninety degrees, and they were all sweating in the large steel bus with no open windows. Kennedy began to think of all those news stories where parents left their babies in the car and they overheated and died. Except this time, they were all adults. Kennedy could see it in the headlines: Twenty Drunk Adults Die from Heatstroke in a Broken-Down Party Bus. Kennedy decided that this was not how she was going to die.

Kennedy walked back up to the front of the bus and started tearing down the black cardboard and tape that was covering the bus windows.

The tiny, half naked stripper started yelling at her from the front seat. "What are you doing? Don't take that down! You'll have to pay for that!"

"What? Does it look like I care?" yelled Kennedy. "It's fucking hot in here, and we're not going anywhere any-time soon! Oh, and I'm not paying for anything! Your fucking bus broke down!" Kennedy continued to tear down the cardboard and open up the windows. The tiny stripper was in tears as everyone followed Kennedy's lead. Within minutes, all of the black cardboard was stripped from the windows, and they were all open. A gust of wind blew through hit the bus. Everyone was able to breathe again.

When Kennedy was done having her argument with the stripper and saving everyone from suffocation, she walked to the back of the bus and took a seat next to Bailey. She noticed Bailey holding a red plastic Solo cup in her hand and staring at it intently.

"I think I'm going to pee in this cup," Bailey told Kennedy.

"What!"

"Kennedy, I have to pee solo bad right now," whined Bailey. Kennedy knew that Bailey was very drunk. Kennedy's eyes scanned around the busy bus.

"Go in the back, behind the stripper's changing curtain," Kennedy told her.

Bailey poured her cup of beer out the window and crawled behind the stripper curtain in the back of the bus. She squatted down and relieved herself in the Solo cup. Kennedy waited for her to return.

Finally, an Atlanta traffic safety squad came to rescue the stranded alcoholics. It took fifteen minutes for the squad to block off three lanes of traffic along I-85. A man dressed in safety gear and a hard hat was coming around the side of the bus to rescue them at about the same time that Bailey was pouring her cup out the window. She did not look before she poured. One of the girls on the bus screamed as Bailey's urine splattered onto the safety officer's leg.

The group was unloaded onto the side of I-85 safely and without casualty. They took photos in front of the bus, which had been towed to the side of the road. They were commemorating their survival of the broken-down party bus. They all called for Ubers and arrived separately, but on time, to see the Boss.

Before going into the arena, Bailey and Kennedy took tequila shots in the parking lot with a couple Kennedy had just met—Courtney and Keith.

"Courtney is the person I was telling you about earlier who did the Year of Yes," said Bailey. "Kennedy is doing a Year of Yes right now," she told Courtney.

"That's awesome! I loved my Year of Yes. It was crazy—I mean, *just nuts*! I met Keith somewhere in my Year of Yes. We met on Tinder. You know what's funny? We went to the same college, and I thought I didn't know him. Then when he texted me after I gave him my number on Tinder, he was already in my contact list! We must have met one night when I was drunk, and I didn't remember him. Ha!"

Kennedy didn't remember much of the Bruce Springsteen concert. The tequila shots had definitely done their job. The next day, when talking on the phone to her dad (who was a giant Bruce Springsteen fan), Kennedy made up a list of songs that Springsteen had sung. She did not tell her parents about the broken-down school bus and the tequila shots. Some stories were better not to share with her parents.

> *The highway's jammed with broken heroes*
> *on a last-chance power drive...*
> *We've gotta get out while we're young,*
> *Because tramps like us,*
> *Baby, we were born to run.*

—The Boss

FIGHTING THE GIANT

Early in April and May, Kennedy joined a kickball team with some coworkers from her office. Kickball was a big deal in Little Rock. Imagine about fifteen hundred people gathering every Sunday to play. There were four different leagues: expert, intermediate, beginner, and laid back. Kennedy's team was in the intermediate league. But everyone on her team played as if they were beginners. They never won a game. David was in the laid-back league. Their teams never cared who won and hardly ever kept score. They also got a lot more intoxicated while playing than the other leagues. The intermediate league, however—they took the game very seriously.

Kennedy joined the office kickball team because it was Year of Yes. Also, she wanted to meet more people in Little Rock. One of the other dentists had volunteered her to be co-captain of the team. The team captains had a few responsibilities. One of them was making sure that nine members of the team were there to play at all times. Another was being assigned to referee some of the games played by other teams. There were specific rules that the captain and the co-captain had to follow when umping. Kennedy had read over the rules a couple of times and was familiar with them from her days of playing as a kid.

The second Sunday in April, the team's captain, Greg, didn't show up. He'd asked if Kennedy could be the main umpire for one of the games. He'd told her that she knew the rules better than the other teammates, who struggled to show up each week. Kennedy asked one of her male teammates to be the ump in the outfield while she stood behind home plate. She had grown up at the baseball fields watching her brothers play. She had also played Whiffle ball in the backyard with her brothers and the neighbors. She knew how to call the plays.

At the start of the game, everything was going smoothly. Kennedy would yell, "Strike," "ball," or "out," and then she would keep score on her clipboard. There were no issues in the beginning of the game.

Then, in the third inning, Kennedy heard someone behind her yelling. "Is that a little girl umping?" yelled the heckler. "Little girls aren't allowed to ump!"

Kennedy turned around to see a giant drunk man. He must have been at least six five and 350 pounds. He was an enormous hulk of a man with biceps and fore-arms that looked to be the circumference of Kennedy's thigh.

"Get out of the game, sweetheart, and come over here! You don't need to be calling the shots!" he said, looking right at her.

Kennedy turned around and went back to the game. She didn't want to miss a call.

The man continued to harass her. "Wrong call, Ump! Get out of the game, sweetie!" the man bellowed. The crowd watching in the bleachers was starting to get very angry with the belligerent man. He was so large, however, that nobody wanted to stand up to him.

Kennedy paused the game between innings. She had the umpire in the outfield come in and take her spot.

She sent a text to David, who was at a different field.

Kennedy: I'm being yelled by a giant for umping.

David: What field?

Kennedy: Field 7.

David: I'll be there soon.

"That's right! Get out of the game, Ump!" yelled the giant.

Kennedy turned around, threw her clip board down hard on the ground behind her, and looked right in the eyes of the man behind the fence. "Why don't you go sit down and be quiet!" she yelled as she pointed her finger at the large man through the wire fence.

"Why don't you suck my dick!" roared the giant.

Then, out of nowhere, four men who were each half the size of the giant grabbed the intoxicated man and dragged him out of the park. The entire crowd was cheering. David was walking up to the field as the men were dragging him out. David, at six two and lean, looked miniature compared to the man they were hauling off.

David's face looked shocked.

"Was that the man pestering you?" he said.

"Yeah, you were a little late. He told me to suck his dick, and then the men on the other team got really angry," said Kennedy.

"I'm not sure I could have taken him out alone," said David.

"I think I could have taken him. No one ever wants to hit a girl," said Kennedy, smiling.

"Kennedy, do you think you'll ever umpire again?" asked David after the game was over.

"Definitely," said Kennedy.

5. MAY

May, she will stay
resting in my arms again.

—*Simon and Garfunkel*

SOUR GUMMIES

The first weekend in May, Kennedy took a weekend trip with her friend Piper to Denver. They planned to stay with Sydney and Trey. David volunteered to keep Rosie for the weekend again. Kennedy was confused about her feelings for David.

Kennedy and Piper had been friends since junior high school. Piper was five feet and ten inches tall with long straight blonde hair and a wide smile. She was a financial advisor in Rogers, Arkansas. They had also been roommates for a couple of years in college.

Sydney, Piper, and Kennedy went out Friday night for dinner. They caught up on one another's lives. The three friends had grown up together and knew one another very well. There was never a moment when they weren't laughing together.

"So how's it going with David the pilot?" asked Sydney.

"You didn't tell me he was a pilot!" said Piper.

"He's an air force pilot. That's different. Also, he's moving at the end of June. So I don't know what is going to become of us. Lately I've been traveling on the weekend. So we basically just keep hanging out during the week."

"When you hang out with him, do you have sex with him?" asked Piper.

"You're so nosey!" said Sydney.

"Most of the time, yes. But it's never just about sex. Sometimes we hang out without having sex," said Kennedy.

"That's so strange. That sounds like dating," said Sydney.

"Well, at least you're getting some action. But I agree, it does sound like you're dating. I mean, unless y'all are seeing other people," said Piper.

"I don't have time to see other people. I don't ask if he's seeing other people. Anyways, I think he's just going to be my transition guy," said Kennedy.

⚊⚊

Piper was fixated on finding and buying at least a small amount of pot – since it was legal in the city limits of Denver. *Yes to smoking marijuana.*

"I just want to see what it's like to buy it! I want to know what a dispensary looks like!" Piper told the girls.

So the next day, after visiting Red Rocks Theater to check out a morning yoga class, the three girls and Trey stopped by a dispensary to buy some weed. There was a line out the door. The small building was packed with all different kinds of customers. Kennedy thought that the funniest customers were the ones who looked her parents' age. She could only imagine what her parents would think if they knew she was purchasing weed. *At least it's legal, so it's within reason*, she thought.

The clerks behind the dispensing counter were very chill as they explained all of the different options of marijuana to the group. They eventually decided on some edible sour-patch gummies and a quarter of an ounce of weed. Then they went back to Sydney and Trey's apartment. They ate the gummies and smoked from Trey's pipe. Neither Kennedy nor Piper had ever smoked marijuana before. Sydney did not smoke or eat a gummy because she was starting a new job in Denver— and she would be drug tested the following Monday before beginning.

They all decided to go out for dinner to one of Trey and Sydney's favorite pizza places. Trey sat in a silent trance, while Piper and Kennedy couldn't stop laughing.

"You know what's really funny?" said Kennedy. "I asked David who his last girlfriend was. He was said she was a Disney princess."

"What? Ha ha. Like at Disney World or is he crazy and actually imagined that he was dating a cartoon character?" asked Piper giggling.

"Yes, Disney Tokyo. When he lived in Japan." Kennedy smiled. Her cheeks were rosy and her eyes squinted. She felt like her face was stuck in a permanent smile. She was nowhere near upset about this.

"That was his last love? I'm not sure you would want to compete with a princess! You should dress up like a princess and show up at his house!" Piper laughed tipping over on her side in the booth.

"I think I would make a good Belle," said Kennedy.

"Guys who are into Disney princesses kind of weird me out. Think about Ariel's boobs. They're just shells. She hardly has any cleavage. No one in real life is actually that perfect. Also, she married a man who didn't hear her speak until the day they wed. That's just asking for a disaster. Ugh. Where is the pizza? I'm getting hungry!" cried Piper.

"She was the smart one, though," Sydney piped in. "She wanted to be part of the human world. She stalked a prince and married him. What better way to join humans than to be a princess?"

"That's true. But she traded her beautiful voice for legs. If the prince didn't take her in, she would have been poorly qualified for any job. Also, she had strange hoarding tendencies that Prince Eric had to deal with," said Piper.

"Look at this stuff, isn't it neat?" sang Piper, waving her fork around in the air.

"I can't handle it," said Kennedy, keeling over in laughter.

That night at dinner, Sydney had to suffer through being the only one in the group that was not high. Kennedy and Piper would start a conversation and completely forget what they were talking about. Later on, Piper would tell the girls that she never thought she had gotten high at all.

David called Kennedy while she was packing her bags that night after dinner.

"I bought a puppy," he told her.

"What? What kind?" she asked. She was surprised. She guessed that keeping Rosie had inspired him to get one of his own.

"It's a Rhodesian ridgeback," said David.

"Wow. Does Rosie like him?" asked Kennedy.

"They seem to be getting along pretty well," said David.

"That's awesome! I didn't even know you wanted a puppy," said Kennedy.

"Yeah, I've been looking into breeders for a while. When are you getting back in town tomorrow?"

"Should be around three p.m., if it doesn't rain. It's supposed to rain tomorrow," said Kennedy.

"Planes fly in the rain, Kennedy," said David.

"Oh, yeah. I forgot you were a pilot. Ha ha. I guess they do fly in the rain."

"Are you okay? You seem...tired."

"Yes, I'm fine. I think I had too many sour-patch gummies," said Kennedy.

"What?"

"Never mind. I'll pick up Rosie tomorrow. Thanks again for keeping her."

"No problem," David replied.

Piper and Kennedy flew back to Arkansas the next day. They drank mimosas in the airport before boarding the plane. Next time, they would make it a longer trip, they told each other as they parted ways.

WRITTEN THERAPY

After picking Rosie up that Sunday, Kennedy didn't hear from David for two weeks. Something had changed. He had gotten a new puppy. But instead of his asking her for advice, there was no communication from him at all. She texted him a couple of times and called once. There was no reply.

Searching for something to take her mind off him, Kennedy remembered what Adrian had said about writing a book. This was the Year of Yes; she might as well say yes to writing a book. So she sat down and started writing.

I remember the day I knew that Sam and I weren't going to make it as a couple. It was the beginning of May, and we were both going to be graduating from dental school at the end of the month. I was on my last rotation back at school in Kansas City, and Sam was in South Carolina on his last dental rotation.

It was a Thursday, and the weather was unusually cold and rainy for May. I had senioritis terribly and was constantly running late. We were so close to graduation; the staff doctors were just happy we showed up to clinic at all.

I was having a particularly bad day. I had spilled coffee all over my white coat that morning. Also, when pulling into the garage after clinic, I shut the garage door on the bumper of my car. I cringed as the garage door squealed and scraped against the rear bumper of my ten-year-old Jetta.

I was living with a classmate named Kelly at the time. We were both engaged. Most of our time was centered around wedding planning and patient care. I made dinner for Kelly that night because she was running late in clinic. We ate dinner in the living room as we watched *Say Yes to the Dress* and planned our weddings. Kelly was getting married in four months, and I was getting married in six.

After dinner, Kelly worked on her wedding registry online while I designed my save-the-date cards on Weddingpaperdivas.com. The website had calculated that the cost would be $430 for three hundred customized cards. That didn't include the magnets that I wanted to order for close friends and family. After adding the finishing touches, I took out the credit card my parents had given me for wedding things and entered the numbers. Unfortunately, the website did not take my type of credit card. I was not about to pay for this myself. I was, at the time, living on nothing but student loans that had to get me through until I found a paying job. So I closed the laptop and started getting ready for bed. Then I called Sam.

"You're going to bed late again," said Sam.

"I know. I was working on our save-the-date cards," I said.

"Oh, gotcha. Did you finish them?"

"For the most part, they're done. I still haven't ordered them, though."

"Oh, cool. How was your day?" asked Sam.

"Not too amazing, I only had two patients show up in clinic today. Oh, and I closed the garage door on the bumper of my car."

"Kennedy, you're such a klutz all the time. It's like you're a walking disaster!"

"That's not fair! It's just been a weird week for me," I said.

"Listen, Kennedy, I've been thinking…maybe you're just too much of a mess for me. I just think we've been fighting so much lately," said Sam.

"What? No, we haven't. We live eighteen hours apart, and we talk every night."

I was in shock.

"Nothing is the same anymore. I think you might be too independent for me. You're just too stubborn. I don't know if both of us being doctors is going to work."

"What? Where is this coming from?" I said, desperately grabbing for something to hold on to.

"I want a wife who will stay home and take care of the kids. I want my wife to be the same religion as I am so that we can go to church together. Also, I don't see what's wrong with having a trophy wife. You seem to hate that idea so much. I just don't think we see eye to eye on things anymore," said Sam.

I should have seen this coming. But, unfortunately, I hadn't. When we were in Atlanta two weeks prior to this, he had said something similar to "I want my wife to be like this." However, we had been drinking heavily. So I had dismissed it. For the last couple of months, we had disagreed on certain issues. But I had been coasting along, planning the wedding as if nothing were wrong.

This time, I realized that he was actually serious. He wanted a Suzy Homemaker. He wanted me to be someone I had never planned on being. I wanted to be successful in my career and have a happy home life with a couple of kids and a dog. However, he did not want the career competition. How had he just discovered this now? How had I never realized that is what he wanted? Surely we had talked over and over about what we wanted our lives together to be like?

I said nothing to fight back. There was only a long, awkward silence on the line. This was the moment I never got over. Even when we tried to fix things. Even when he supported me through a very difficult time. This was the moment I never got over. This was the moment I fell out of love with him.

Let me just say that there are women who want to stay at home. Women who do amazing jobs raising their children and keeping their houses sane and clean while their husbands work. They develop hobbies and friendships, and they work for charities. They do make a difference. But this wasn't me. He was telling me that he wanted a wife who wasn't me and he had already put a ring on my finger. I felt doomed.

Finally Sam said, "Kennedy?"

There was a stale, awkward silence. Then I hung up the phone on him.

My whole body was shaking. I went to the bathroom to grab some tissues. I slumped down on the floor and began weeping. Four years and an engagement. How could he say such awful things? Why couldn't he love me for who I was instead of the imaginary wife he wanted me to be? Furthermore, what century were we in?

I was devastated. Sam might as well have said, "We're over; I don't love you anymore." All I could think about was how trophies sit on shelves and get dusty while men go out and collect more. I did not plan on being a dusty trophy.

I cried myself to sleep that night. The next day, Sam called me and acted as if everything were normal. The following day, I called my parents and told them that we were postponing the wedding. We continued to see each other and tried to patch things up, but that night was the beginning of a seven-month breakup.

Kennedy stopped typing and closed her laptop. It was too sad a story, she thought. Also, with that beginning, they would only see Sam as the villain. Sam had been her best friend. The reader wouldn't know that she and Sam had had an amazing three and a half years together before it all went downhill. Maybe they were two people who connected for a brief moment in their lives when they had school and graduating in common and didn't notice they they were growing and changing into the people they were to become.

Oh I don't know what you've been told
But this gal right here's gonna rule the world
Yeah that is where I'm gonna be because I wanna be
No I don't wanna sit still, look pretty

-Daya

FAKE NAMES AND
FAKE GAMES

The last Thursday in May, Kennedy decided to reopen the Tinder app that she had downloaded when she was in New York visiting Jenna. She matched with a man named Bow Bow. There were four fun photos of him in New York City. His tagline read, "Just moved here from New York City." A New Yorker in Little Rock; that was funny to think about. Kennedy swiped right. *It was a match.*

Bow Bow: Hi, I'm Michael.
Kennedy: I'm Kennedy. Where did Bow Bow come from?
Bow Bow: It's a nickname that my friends call me.

Kennedy: Gotcha. Why are you moving here from New York City? Are you originally from here?

Bow Bow: No, I'm coming here for a medical residency program. I'm from NYC originally.

Kennedy: Wow, how low on the residency match list was Little Rock for you? I'm guessing it wasn't your top pick.

Bow Bow: Ha ha, yeah, it was pretty low on the list. I didn't see it coming when I matched. You must be in the medical field. Are you a nurse or something?

Kennedy: I'm a dentist. What are you doing your residency in?

Bow Bow: Neurology and neurosurgery. It's a really competitive field. That's how I ended up here. Are you from here originally?

Kennedy: I'm an Arkansas native, but I'm from northwest Arkansas.

Bow Bow: I see. How long have you lived in Little Rock?

Kennedy: Five months.

Bow Bow: So you know your way around here pretty well, then?

Kennedy: Yes, I do.

Bow Bow: Any interest in showing me around tonight in Little Rock? I'll buy you dinner and drinks.

Kennedy: It sounds like a lot of fun. I could show you where to go out on Thursday nights. I will tell you, though, I don't do Tinder hookups. I'm more of a three-date kind of a girl.

Bow Bow: No problem. That's respectable. I'm just looking for dinner and drinks in a new city with a sexy lady. Where do people go on Thursday nights?

Kennedy: Cajuns is always busy on Thursdays. Also, they have an awesome patio that would be great in this weather.

Bow Bow: Perfect. Do you want to meet there at 8:00 tonight?

Kennedy: Sounds good. But first, I need your last name.

Bow Bow: What? Why?

Kennedy: So I can verify that who I'm meeting up with is a legitimate person. Why are you even questioning this?

Bow Bow: I'm afraid I can't tell you my last name. But we will be meeting in public. So it will be safe.

Kennedy: I can't go if I don't know your last name.

Bow Bow: But we'll be meeting in public.

Kennedy: This isn't New York City. In New York, you walk out of your apartment and you're in public. There are people EVERYWHERE. But things are different here. It is not that safe.

Bow Bow: I understand, I guess. I don't think you're crazy for not going out with me.

Kennedy: I know I'm not crazy for not meeting you out. Little Rock is not safe for women. This city is known for women getting murder-raped. You could be the next Craigslist killer—or I guess Tinder killer. Also, the fact that your real name isn't on your profile and you won't give me your last name—that just screams married.

Bow Bow: Well, here's my number if you ever re-consider. 555-365-4418.

The next day, Kennedy opened up her Tinder account again. She had received a photo message from Bow Bow. In his photo he was naked and holding his penis in front of the mirror. *Nice abs, but creepy as hell*, thought Kennedy as she shook her head.

SECOND PROPOSAL

The last Saturday in May, Kennedy went to Cajun's Wharf with her friends Robyn, Sarah, and Tyler. Kennedy was having a guy meet her out at the bar. She had met him on one of the dating websites she had been perusing. His name was Eric. The three things she liked about him were that he liked to run, he had a dog, and he was an engineer.

Eric made eye contact with her at the bar and introduced himself. He was several inches taller than Kennedy, with short brown and bright green eyes. He also had three-day stubble and wore a neat pressed blue shirt. Eric bought Kennedy a drink and they talked for a while about Little Rock and what they liked to do there.

They chatted about what they did in their free time. They both talked about their dogs and how tough it was raising a puppy.

Halfway through the conversation, Eric's friend Mikey showed up next to him at the bar. He was clearly intoxicated. Mikey had blonde spiked hair. He was also short but yet he was broad shouldered, with muscles popping out of his tight V-neck shirt. He clearly spent a lot of time at the gym. He was drunkenly catcalling every girl who walked by. Then Kennedy and Eric watched him try to pick a fight with another muscle-bound man who walked by him. Eric grabbed him before anything could start.

"I'm sorry; I'm going to have to go. My friend is too out of control, and I need to get him home," said Eric.

"It's okay. I understand. It was nice to meet you," said Kennedy.

"It was great to meet you too. Maybe I can take you on a date sometime."

"That's sounds great. You have my number." Kennedy watched Eric hold his drunken friend around the waist as he escorted him out of the bar.

She started to look around to see where the friends she had come with were. Then a familiar face caught her eye at the bar—it was David.

"I saw that your friend checked you in on Facebook here. I thought I would come say hi," said David.

"You haven't called me back in two weeks. Why are you here?" said Kennedy.

"I know. I'm very sorry. Mufasa was sick, and I had to nurse him back to health. Also, I've been incredibly busy with flight training."

"I have a puppy too. I could have helped you. A text message would have been nice. But no, you just show up here, unannounced," said Kennedy, raising her voice to be heard over the band that was now playing onstage.

"Look, I'm really sorry. I have no good excuse for my absence. But I do know that I like you, and I want to hang out with you," said David. "Let me buy you a drink to apologize."

Kennedy didn't believe David's excuse. But she was tipsy and willing to let him hang out with her again anyway. He led her to the dance floor, and they danced to the band. Then they introduced his friends to her friends.

"Where did David come from? Where did Eric go?" asked Robyn, confused at the change in beaus.

"Eric had to take his drunken friend home. Then David showed up because you tagged us here on Facebook."

"Oh, I'm sorry about that...I think? Wait, did you want him to show up? Are you upset? I didn't realize you two were still hanging out," said Robyn.

"Yeah, me neither," said Kennedy.

"David seems really nice, though! He's cute, too! I'd definitely hit that until he left. But his friend kind of seems like an asshole," said Robyn.

"Yeah, that's Carl. I'm not sure what to think about him. He's a pilot too. I think he sent me a weird message on OkCupid once," said Kennedy.

At the end of the night, Carl drove David and Kennedy back to her townhouse. Kennedy and David were both heavily intoxicated. In the truck, Kennedy found Carl's helmet and flight mask. She put them on and started pretending to be a pilot.

"Buzz, buzz, ten-four, over and out...roger that, Captain. The plane is going down!" She was cracking herself up. The men were laughing at her. Probably not with her.

Back at her townhouse, Kennedy was using the downstairs bathroom while David played fetch with Rosie in the living room.

"We should get married," said David from the living room.

"What? What did you say?" yelled Kennedy while she was sitting on the toilet.

"We should get married," said David again, only a fraction louder than before.

Kennedy flushed the toilet, washed her hands, and walked out of the bathroom. She was livid.

"We should get married?" she said as she looked at him in puzzlement. "We are not getting married!" Kennedy yelled as she pointed her finger at the handsome pilot.

"First of all, I was on the toilet when you said that. That was wrong. Second of all, I haven't heard from you in two weeks! Two *fucking* weeks! It's like you think I'm just sitting around waiting for you to come and sweep me off my feet! Well, I have news for you. I have a life too, and if you want to be in it, you have to fucking keep in contact with me!"

Kennedy and David had the best drunken sex of their skewed relationship that night. Afterward, they still did not define the relationship. But David did start calling again, every day.

6. JUNE

June, she'll change her tune.
In restless walks she'll prowl the night.

—*Simon and Garfunkel*

SUMMER FLING

In the past few weeks, Kennedy had been spending her Sundays going to the pool in her small townhouse complex. It was the best was to beat the humid heat of a Little Rock summer. She was usually there alone with her book. Most of the people in the townhouses around her were elderly people. She preferred it that way. They were always home and always in her business. She felt safe that they were there. Regardless, elderly people did not use the pool much on Sunday afternoon.

She walked to the pool with her towel and *Last Chance Saloon* in her hands. This day was different. There were several, at least six, men at her pool. This surprised her.

She walked in cautiously and spread her towel out on the only open lounge chair.

After she had been lounging for about ten minutes, one of the men at the pool offered her a beer. They were drinking Michelob Ultra—her favorite. Of course, she said yes. She walked to the side of the small pool and dipped her feet into it.

"I'm Kennedy, by the way," she said. "Thanks for the beer."

"No problem. I'm Michael. That's Craig."

"Hi!" said Craig.

"That's Tony on the raft, Justin is the one asleep on the chair, and Kyle and Mason just went to go and get more beer. I don't expect you to remember all of our names. Do you live in this complex?" asked Michael.

"Yes, I do. Do any of you live in this complex?" Kennedy asked hesitantly but trying to be friendly.

"Mason does. We're all friends of Mason," said Craig.

"Actually, I'm Mason's boyfriend," said Michael.

It was clicking in Kennedy's head. They were all gay. This made so much since. There was no way she would find a pool full of gorgeous men in Little Rock without all of them being gay. She suddenly felt at ease with her new friends. She grabbed a raft and started floating around the pool. They talked a lot. She found out a lot about them in a very short time. Two of them, Tony and Justin, were in law school. Mason and Kyle were both lawyers, and Michael was a physical therapist.

"Are you dating anyone right now?" Michael asked.

"Well, I'm sort of dating an air force pilot. But he's leaving. So I don't think we're going to stay together," said Kennedy.

"So you're having a fling?" asked Craig.

"Not exactly. He does take me on dates." Kennedy laughed.

"'Dating a pilot' is like just a nice way to say, 'I'm sleeping with a pilot.' You don't really date pilots," said Craig.

"He's right, you know. I dated a pilot once. He was amazing and beautiful. He took me to Las Vegas, and we partied all night for a long weekend. He wasn't a keeper, though. I know that he cheated on me constantly. I didn't like him that much. Let's just call that a fling too," said Michael.

"I don't know if it's a fling," said Kennedy.

Kennedy left the pool more confused than ever about her relationship with David. Should she even be defining a relationship with him? Did she love him? Did he love her? He did propose to her, but he was wasted, and she was on the toilet. She was just enjoying his company at the time. That was the first time she had asked herself if she saw a future with him. She honestly did not know.

MEETING MOM

Kennedy was out for a run with Rosie on the following Thursday afternoon when David called. She stopped running and answered the call on the headphones she was listening to music on.

"Hey, what's up?" she said.

"Not too much. What are you doing right now?" asked David.

"I'm out for a run with Rosie. Why?"

"Do you think you could be ready to go to dinner at seven thirty?" asked David.

Kennedy checked her watch; it was six o'clock. "Umm…maybe? Are you asking me to dinner then?"

"My mom's in town. I want you to meet her."

"This is definitely short notice David."

"Please come and meet her. She'll love you," pleaded David.

Yes, to meeting the mom? Kennedy asked herself.

Kennedy ran home with Rosie and jumped in the shower. She put on a casual summer sundress, a little bit of makeup, and headed out the door. Was it too soon to meet his parents? She didn't remember the protocol.

When she showed up at the restaurant, David, Thomas, Carl, and David's mother, Vicki were all seated at a table near the corner window. They ordered beer and talked until the food arrived. Vicki asked Kennedy about being a dentist. Kennedy described her office culture, shared a story about one of the crazy hygienists on staff and gave her some electric toothbrush and mouthwash suggestions.

Kennedy ordered a pear salad. It came on a bed of spinach leaves with goat cheese, pears, cranberries, pecans, and grilled chicken. She took one bite and realized that the salad was warm. In fact, it was so warm that the feta was melting on the salad. She nudged David. "This salad is very warm."

"What? Warm? That's strange," said David.

"Warm? Oh, I thought you said it was boring!" said David's mom. "I was thinking I would never invite you to my house and make salad."

"Ha ha, no," said Kennedy. "I just think it's odd. Salad should be served cold, right?"

"David, be a man and ask the waitress if she can bring Kennedy another salad," said Vicki.

"Excuse me, miss," said David to the waitress. "My friend's salad was served warm, and we don't think it should be warm."

"You're right. It shouldn't be warm. I will bring a new one right away," said the waitress.

When Kennedy's salad came back, it was nice and crisp. She started poking her fork around in the salad to eat it. Then she felt her fork hit something hard and make a clinking noise. Kennedy moved the lettuce around and pulled a large metal spoon out.

"Oh my gosh, I just found a large spoon in my salad!" said Kennedy, laughing.

"That's crazy!" said David's mom.

"Excuse me, miss!" said David, trying to grab the waitress's attention again.

"I can do it this time. It's fine," said Kennedy

"Yes?" said the waitress.

"I don't know how it happened, but I just found a large metal spoon in my salad."

"Oh, no! I'm so, so sorry! I will get you another one right away," said the waitress.

"I'm not even sure I want another salad," replied Kennedy.

"You won't be charged for the salad at all," said the waitress.

The group had a good laugh, but took care of the waitress who was obviously stressed over the issue. After dinner by going to the Rev Room for karaoke night. David sang his favorite Frank Sinatra song, "Summer

Winds." Kennedy sang "Love Song" by Sara Bareilles. Then she showed David's mom how to do the Cupid Shuffle. They spent the night laughing and dancing on the patio.

The next day, after work, Kennedy and David loaded up Mufasa and Rosie into David's land cruiser. They headed out to hike Pinnacle Mountain. With the windows open and the music playing, Kennedy was watching Rosie's and Mufasa's ears blow in the wind.

They were pulling to a rolling stop in the camp parking lot when Kennedy saw Rosie, through the rearview mirror, jump out of the window of the moving vehicle. Kennedy screamed and jumped out of the car too. Rosie had landed on all four feet and took off up the path through the woods. This puppy was not scared of anything. Kennedy called her to come back, but Rosie definitely wasn't listening. She followed her up the trail. But Rosie was so fast, there was no catching her. When Kennedy finally caught sight of her, a little boy on the trail was petting Rosie.

"Can you just hold on to that dog for me?" asked Kennedy. "Thanks!" she said as she dragged Rosie back down the trail to David and Mufasa.

"Seat belt," said Kennedy. "I'm getting her a seat belt."

"She also needs training classes. She shouldn't want to run away from you like that," said David.

"The woes of being a dog mom," said Kennedy as she and David started up the trail. This time with both dogs on leads.

"Speaking of moms, mine really liked you," said David. "She was very impressed."

"She was very fun to hang out with. I think she was a little disappointed I was a Democrat, though. But she seems like an awesome lady."

"I think she'll get over that. Or at least hope you'll change your mind."

"Good luck with that one," replied Kennedy.

They climbed to the top of Pinnacle just before the sun began to slip below the horizon. David talked to Kennedy about his family and what it was like growing up in Colorado. Then they sat and watched the sun slowly sink into the other side of the world.

"This is my favorite spot in Little Rock," said Kennedy.

David squeezed his arm around her shoulder. "This is my favorite spot in Little Rock." Then he kissed her lightly on the forehead. "But we have to get down this mountain before it's pitch black." He smiled.

"Good thinking," said Kennedy.

The summer wind came blowin' in from across the sea.
It lingered there to touch your hair and walk with me.
All summer long we sang a song, and then we strolled that golden sand,
Two sweethearts and the summer wind.

—Frank Sinatra

SAYING GOOD-BYE

I t was the last week in June, and the days were getting
longer and more humid. David the pilot was moving. He asked her to come over after work to help pack
things up. Kennedy put on her favorite tank top and
ratty jean shorts, loaded Rosie into her car, and headed
to David's house.

Kennedy tried not to focus too much on the moving part. She knew he was her transition man. She had
known he was going to leave when she met him. They
had only known each other four months. *It's just that the
last few weeks had been so nice*, she thought.

She picked up some Greek food from one of her
favorite restaurants to take to David's house. When

she arrived, she put Rosie in the backyard to play with Mufasa. Then she went outside to see David. He was pushing a large dresser up the ramp of a U-Haul. He was covered in sweat.

"Are you working alone?" Kennedy asked.

"Yes. I sent out a message on Facebook to my air force buddies here and asked for help. No one has replied," he said while still working.

"What about your brother?" Kennedy asked.

"He hasn't been home since this morning. He didn't work today. I don't know where the hell he is. He's not answering his phone," said David as he wiped sweat from his forehead.

"That's really strange. Why is his car here if he's not?"

"I'm not sure, but can I ask you to pack up the stuff in the kitchen? There are already boxes ready to go."

Kennedy was packing up the boxes in the kitchen when she heard David talking to someone in the front yard. It was a scraggly-looking man in an old S-10 pickup truck. Kennedy walked out the front door to listen to the conversation. The man was a picker. He was asking David if he wanted to get rid of any of his things. David gave him two hubcaps from the car he used to have and a couple of damaged air force posters. In return, the picker gave David an old miniature grandfather clock. It was at the end of the clock's life, but David took it anyway.

"Thank you so much for your trade! Those hubcaps will go a long way!" said the picker. "That's one hot momma of a lady you have there too! We could do a trade for her too."

David laughed in his funny way and said, "That won't be happening, sir. Have a nice day." He smiled largely, stuck his hand in the air, and waved good-bye.

Later, while they were eating the Greek food on the floor in the empty living room, another car pulled up outside. This time it was a car carrying Thomas.

Thomas stumbled into the living room. It was six thirty in the afternoon, and he was wasted. He was fumbling around, and he could not make a coherent sentence.

"Thomas, where have you been?" asked David.

"Meh, Robet an I wen to the riva…" Thomas stumbled to his room, where he passed out on the floor next to his bed.

"Is he going to be okay?" asked Kennedy.

David looked angry; his eyes darkened. "He's my brother. He knew I was moving today. You'd think that out of all the people who were supposed to help me move, he would be the one to show up semi sober!"

Kennedy helped with what she could. She played music on her phone as she packed up what was left of the kitchen utensils. Then she sat with Mufasa and Rosie and watched David pack up the rest of the U-Haul. She felt a little twitch in her eyes. It surprised her that she was fighting back tears. She had not known this man for very long—four months was not long. But he had become part of her new life in Little Rock. She was going to miss him terribly. But Kennedy was stubborn, and she wasn't about to tell him that she was sad.

David slept in her bed that night. He had parked the U-Haul outside of her house. They cuddled together but did nothing more than that. She was too sad, and he was too tired.

He woke up early in the morning and said good-bye to her. She gave him a hug and kiss. That was all. She did not cry until she made it back to her bed. He was just her transition man; she shouldn't be upset, she thought.

And in the morning I'll be with you,
But it will be a different kind.
'Cause I'll be holding all the tickets,
And you'll be owning all the fines.

—Birdy

7. JULY

July, she will fly
and give no warnings of her flight.

—Simon and Garfunkel

NEW ROOMMATE

"I'm just calling to tell you that I don't want to be involved in this living situation!" David yelled over the phone.

"What do you mean?" Kennedy asked. Her cell coverage was spotty and she could barely hear him.

"I mean, if you and Thomas get into a fight or if he is being a terrible roommate, I don't want to hear about it. You're just going to have to man up and be his landlord. Don't come crying to me! I do not want to have anything to do with this!"

Beep...beep...beep...Kennedy had lost cell service. She was driving through the Ozark Mountains on a trek to Sarah and Drew's mountain home in the woods.

"Perfect time to lose cell signal...What a jerk," said Kennedy out loud to Rosie, who was huddled in the passenger seat of the car. Kennedy was angry and at a loss as to why he was being so awful. After all, she was doing his younger brother a favor. The kid didn't have anywhere to stay.

⚓

"Did Captain Dave profess his undying love to you before he left?" asked Sarah as they were fixing the vegetable for dinner that night.

"Nothing close to that," said Kennedy. "He was a total jerk about his brother being my roommate."

"That's not good. Are you okay?"

"I'll be fine," Kennedy replied as she continued to dice the tomatoes.

Three days before, Kennedy had been preparing for this trip to the mountains after David had left. She had messaged David and asked him if she could have the cooler that he had left behind for her float trip. He had said yes and told her to take anything else she wanted in the house as well.

When she went to pick up the cooler, Thomas was there. He was cleaning things up, very slowly. What was left in the house was in complete disarray. There were items strewn all over the place. It was clear he still had a long way to go. Kennedy grabbed the cooler, three large wine glasses, and the Japanese cat clock that David had encouraged her to take.

Before she left, Thomas stopped her and asked her the inevitable question. "Kennedy, the friend that I'm supposed to be staying with bailed on me. I have no place to live. Do you think I could rent out your guest bedroom until I find a new place to live?"

There was hesitation in his voice. "It won't be for very long, and I'll pay you rent," said Thomas.

Year...of...Yes, thought Kennedy. *Within reason...*

"I'll give you a month," replied Kennedy. She had no idea what she was getting into.

NEGOTIATIONS

It was the second Monday in July. Kennedy had a big day ahead of her. She was negotiating her contract with the business partners of her dental office. Her six-month trial period was complete. She decided that she did not want to become a partner. She would remain an employee. She wasn't sure if Little Rock was where she wanted to be grounded forever or not.

Kennedy had presented a salary figure to the business manager. A figure that she thought she deserved. This figure would be enough to help her pay off her student loans and still live comfortably. She thought it was a reasonable figure, considering her ex-fiancé, Sam, was making $10,000 more than that in a tiny town in

North Carolina. Also, it was an amount that would make her want to stay in Little Rock. At least for the next few years, she thought. This was her first time negotiating a contract. She was very nervous.

The day did not go as planned. As soon as she arrived at the office, she overheard the partners in the practice discussing how much they were going to offer her. She could hear them talking through the wall of her office. Kennedy felt unbelievably embarrassed that she could hear them talking. But somehow, she could not stop listening to the conversation. This was not a meeting; the partners had already had the main meeting. These were just two of the male doctors in the practice discussing the logistics of the meeting they just had and the decision they had made.

She heard one of the older male doctors complaining that she had asked for too much money. This was the doctor with whom Kennedy had her biggest issues. He was constantly belittling her and her ability to do her job. Kennedy blamed it on the generation gap. He was one of the oldest doctors in her practice, and she was the youngest. He was always nice to her face. However, he was continually persistent about how she should date his son. Also, on two occasions, he had made jokes about wanting to see her in her bikini.

She opened up her e-mail, and there it was. The e-mail with her offer in it. There were two offers presented to her. The first was a fixed salary that was $13,000 less than what she had asked for. The second was $25,000 less than what she had asked for, but it gave her a bonus for each patient she saw over a specified number.

Kennedy was deflated. She did not reply to the e-mail offer that day. She saw the patients on her schedule. Then she left without saying a word about the contract or the offer to anyone.

On her way home, she called her dad to tell him what was going on. She broke down in tears. He handled the situation far better than she had thought he would. He told her to forward him the e-mail. Then they would talk it through.

Kennedy wasn't just upset because it wasn't the amount she wanted. She was upset because she had spent the last few months thinking that she was going to get more than she'd just been offered. She had gone on all those trips and was paying low amounts on her credit card, waiting for her raise. Also, her parents were still helping her pay her students loans. Once her pay went up, she would not need them to do that. But now her income would not increase enough for her to take on the loans and pay off her significant amount of credit-card debt. The Year of Yes had started to take a toll on her bank account.

"They obviously lowballed me. If I were a single parent, with my student loans, I couldn't support my child right now. If I were a man, I would have received an offer at least $15,000 higher. I hate this!" Kennedy found herself saying over the phone as tears ran down her cheeks.

Kennedy's dad had a difficult time consoling her. He had worked tremendously hard to become the successful owner of an architecture firm. However, at her age, he had been making a fraction of the salary she was currently being offered.

When Kennedy arrived at her townhouse, she got of her car and sat down by the swimming pool. No one was ever at the pool after she got off of work. It was a nice, quiet place to cry. Besides, she knew Thomas would be at her house, and she didn't want to talk to him.

David had called while she was on the phone to her dad. He had left a message to get back with her. She sent him a text message saying, "I have had a rough day. I do not want to talk right now."

David called again, twice. The second time, Kennedy picked up the phone. She was still sitting on a lounger by the pool in her work scrubs.

"What do you want?" said Kennedy in a harsh tone. She was still remembering the last conversation they had had before Thomas had moved in with her.

"Is Thomas at the house?" asked David.

"I'm not sure. I haven't made it home yet. He was at the house at lunch. I didn't see him, but his car was there, and his door was shut. Why do you ask?"

"My parents are trying to get ahold of him. He hasn't answered his phone since Saturday," said David.

Kennedy thought his tone of voice sounded more annoyed than concerned.

Thomas had been living in Kennedy's guest room for a full week and a half. He had been at the lake with his friends the previous weekend. Kennedy had talked to him the night before. Earlier that day, she had come home from lunch and noticed his car was still there. She had noted the door to his room was still closed. It was noon, and she was sure he was still asleep.

"I'll let you know when I get to the townhouse if he's there," said Kennedy, and she hung up the phone.

She got off the lounger at the pool and walked over to her townhouse. Thomas's car was still there. He was most likely still in his room. She walked up the stairs and knocked on the door to his bedroom. There was no answer. Then she tried opening the door to his bedroom. It was locked. At this point, she went to Rosie, who was whining in her kennel, and let her out to go to the bathroom.

She went back to Thomas's bedroom door one more time and yelled, "Thomas! Your parents have been trying to call you!" She banged on the door a couple more times. There was still no answer.

Kennedy went downstairs to the kitchen and realized she had no food in the house. She decided that this would be an ideal time to go to the grocery store. She would try one more time to wake up Thomas when she got back. He was probably still sleeping from his long weekend at the lake.

Kennedy called David as she walked to the grocery store.

"I think Thomas is in his room sleeping. His car has been parked outside all day, and the door to his room is locked," she told David.

"How has it been? Living with him?" asked David.

"I thought you didn't want to know," Kennedy said smugly.

"I was being an asshole when I said that," said David. "Does he keep the house clean? Does he help with chores?"

"Umm...He's not here a lot. When he is, he keeps the common areas clean for the most part. He helped me take out the trash the other day. But his room is a complete mess and kind of smells like hemp. Also, for some reason, every time he sits down, nuts and bolts fall out of his pockets. I guess that has to do with him being a carpenter. I'm not sure."

"This is just incomprehensible! I'm so sorry my little brother is just squatting in your house," said David.

"On the other hand, he's hardly here when I'm here. He also lets Rosie out when she needs to go out and I'm not here."

"Well, he shouldn't have asked to stay with you in the first place. I feel responsible for letting this happen. I also think he took advantage of your kindness and your guest bedroom. I'm going to call my parents and tell them that."

Then Kennedy asked David the question that had been on everyone's mind.

"David, are you afraid I'm going to sleep with your little brother?"

Click. David had hung up the phone already.

THE DOWNFALL

Just a few minutes later, Kennedy was meandering through the aisles of the grocery store when her phone rang. The caller ID said it was an unknown number from Colorado. She picked up the phone and answered with a questioning "Hello?"

"Hi, is this Kennedy? This is Vicki, David's mom. We met when I came in town to visit the boys."

"Yes, I remember meeting you! How are you?" said Kennedy, a little confused as to why she was calling.

"I'm doing well. However, I'm a little concerned about Thomas. I haven't been able to contact him since Saturday. David said he's been drinking a lot lately. He also said that Thomas has been locked in his room at your house."

"Yes, ma'am. He was still in there when I left. He didn't respond when I tried yelling through the door."

"Do you mind trying again? I'm very concerned about him."

"I'm at the grocery store right now, but I can when I get back to the townhouse," said Kennedy.

"Okay. Well, I'll tell you, I'm extremely concerned about him. David's father wants to talk to you," said Vicki.

"Kennedy?" came the voice of David's father over the phone. "This is Ron, David's father. I heard that Thomas is locked in your guest room."

"Yes. Yes, he is," replied Kennedy.

"Well, the reason I'm really concerned about him is pretty serious. This time last year, you see, one of his friends was hit by a car at an antiabortion rally. And his friend was killed by that car. Thomas is only twenty-one, and I'm terribly concerned about him being depressed," said Ron.

After talking with Ron Knox on the phone, Kennedy decided to leave her almost-empty grocery cart in the aisle and hurry home. *What have I gotten myself into?* she thought as she was briskly walking the three blocks back to her townhouse. She felt very bad for Thomas. This whole situation was a mess.

She returned to the townhouse and tried banging on Thomas's door again.

There was still no answer.

This time, she was starting to worry. What if Thomas had committed suicide in her guest bedroom? The thought took a while to sink in. She didn't know him very well. He was just the younger brother of David, the pilot she had dated on and off for three or four months. He had been David's sidekick when David was in town. She knew he was young, he liked to drink a lot, and he went to Saint Andrew's Cathedral on Wednesday and Sunday nights. He didn't have a girlfriend. He had one friend, Jake, who had several tattoos and a Mohawk. That was really all she knew about him.

Kennedy tried again to yell and bang on the door. There was still no reply. She called Thomas's parents back.

"I can't get him to respond through the door," said Kennedy.

"I think you should call 911. They'll be able to open the door for you," said Ron Knox.

Ten minutes later, sirens were wailing, and a fire truck was outside of Kennedy's townhouse. There were five firemen on the truck. She showed the men upstairs to open the door. The firemen kicked the door in, and there was Thomas. He was lying on his bed, fully clothed, and not under the covers. Kennedy sprang forward to check for a pulse.

It was there! Thomas was breathing. He was just unconscious. The firemen called for an ambulance. Minutes later, Thomas was being put into the back of an ambulance on a stretcher.

"Do you want to ride with your husband to the hospital?" one of the EMTs asked Kennedy.

"I'll just meet him there. Thanks," Kennedy muttered, shaking all over.

Kennedy sat on her front stoop and watched as the ambulance pulled away. She then called David's parents to give them an update. Vicki picked up the phone.

"Your son is on his way to the hospital. He's still breathing, with a pulse, but he was unconscious. He most likely has alcohol poisoning. I'm sorry I didn't think to get to him sooner," said Kennedy. She used her patient-adapted doctor voice.

A week later, when Thomas was back to normal and still alive, Kennedy told him that he had to move out by the end of the month. This gave him two weeks to find a place.

"I understand," said Thomas. "But promise that you'll keep in touch with my brother, okay?"

"I'll try," said Kennedy.

Thomas bought a camper and moved to a trailer park somewhere in the city. Later, his name showed up on her patient schedule multiple times. Each time he did not show up for his appointment. Once, when he did show up, the front desk could not get his insurance verified. Kennedy never saw him. However, the technicians told her that he was a scraggly man who looked as if he hadn't bathed in a while.

8. AUGUST

August, die she must,
The autumn winds blow chilly and cold.

—Simon and Garfunkel

THE TEST

It had been a week since Thomas had moved out of Kennedy's townhouse. She had just finished with her run with Rosie when David texted her to ask if she wanted to FaceTime. "Give me thirty minutes," she told him. Then she spent thirty minutes trying to look better than she did but still as natural as possible.

When he showed up on her iPad, he was sitting at his kitchen table. He was wearing his flight suit and drinking what Kennedy assumed was whiskey and water.

"Well, hello there, miss," he said. He asked about her weekend in Kansas City and what all she had done there. She asked about his weekend as well. After the Thomas incident, they had started talking again, every day.

After some small talk, David took a drink of his whiskey and set it down on the table. With a serious look on his face, he said, "Kennedy, why do you keep talking to me?"

"What do you mean?" Kennedy asked.

"I mean, I expected you to find another guy right after I left. I mean, that's what typically happens," said David.

"Well, it was kind of difficult with your brother living here," replied Kennedy.

Kennedy thought for a minute. She laughed to herself about how Carl had sent her a Facebook message asking her for her number and a date.

She said, "To be honest, I've been going on dates and talking to other guys. It's just...easier to talk to you. We've already established something. Maybe I'm having a little difficulty letting it go. Also, you are guilty of still talking to me as well. I feel like this goes both ways."

"Kennedy...Do you like me? A lot?" asked David.

"David, I hate to say this, but I have yet to find a guy that I like to kiss as much as you. Or that I can talk to as easily. Personally, I find this very frustrating. Mainly because you don't live here, and you will not live here ever again. Also, we don't agree on a lot of things. But somehow, we always manage to understand each other. It's not that I don't want to go on awesome adventures with you. It's not that I'm against moving. It's just that I've already moved for a man. Then, when I moved for him, he wanted me to turn into a person that I was not."

"I see how this could be a dilemma for you," said David.

"But the most confusing part of it all is that when I ended my four-year relationship, I did not cry one tear in the end. And you...you...I've only known you for four months. I cried when you left. You didn't see it, but I cried. Yeah, I cried! This is so frustrating!"

"I'm going to be honest with you, Kennedy," said David. "I could always see a future with you."

There was a long pause on both ends.

"Then I think the logical thing to do is to try dating long distance and see how it goes," said Kennedy, finally.

David was very excited about this. He told her he wanted her to fly to Albuquerque in the next couple of weeks. Kennedy said she couldn't take any more time off of work. She had already used all of her vacation days. Plus, she was still low on funds as a result of her poor contract negotiation skills. But, mainly, she wanted him to come to her. It was a test. If he was serious about her, he would come to her.

"Don't you get a military discount when you fly? You are a pilot, right?" asked Kennedy.

"Yes, but I don't know if I can get off for a weekend. I'll see if I can get the last flight out next Friday," said David.

Kennedy and David talked on Skype every night for the next two weeks. They talked about anything and everything. They talked about their future, what they wanted out of life. David also gave Kennedy advice on how to handle the crazy dental hygienist and other staff-related issues that she was having at work.

When the following Friday arrived, David called and said he couldn't come. His Land Cruiser needed fixing. He could not get on a flight. He had to spend the weekend working on his Land Cruiser.

After he gave her this excuse, Kennedy knew. Flying to Little Rock to come see her would have been the grand gesture to kick off their relationship. It would have been a weekend sacrifice for him. He had failed the test. If he would not commit to one weekend visit that inconvenienced him, he was not worth moving for.

"Kennedy, I'm sorry. I just can't do it," David had said.

"David, I feel like if you really cared, you would actually be here. This was it. If you wanted this, you would be here. You dropped the ball. You're not here. I don't feel like talking to you for a while." Kennedy hung up the phone.

Like painted kites, those days and nights, they went flyin' by
The world was new beneath a blue umbrella sky
Then softer than a piper man one day it called to you
I lost you, I lost you to the summer wind

—Frank Sinatra

LAST CHANCE SALOON

Kennedy was disappointed that David didn't make it to Little Rock that weekend. She spent Friday night at home watching a Netflix marathon of *Orange Is the New Black* with Rosie. She also polished off a half pint of TCBY mint chocolate chip frozen yogurt.

She woke up early Saturday morning and went to yoga class. She and Rosie then went to the farmers' market downtown. Then she took Rosie to the dog park with the book her mom had given her.

She walked around the dog park, following Rosie for a little bit. Then she found a seat on one of the benches in the middle of the park. There were what looked like two couples sitting on the benches next to her. Rosie played with their dogs for a little bit.

The man sitting closest to her pointed at Rosie, turned to her, and said, "Your dog looks like a teddy bear. What kind is it?" he asked.

"She's an Irish terrier. It's similar to an Airedale, but smaller," said Kennedy. "Which dog is yours?"

"Well, I don't have a dog here. I'm actually here with my mom and my sister and her boyfriend. That small cavapoo over there is my mom's dog, Peter, and the German shepherd is my sister's boyfriend's dog, Champ. Those two mutts over there, Steve and Frida, are rescues that my mom is fostering. My mom is part of the underground dog rescue railroad," he said with a smile.

"What's the underground dog rescue?" asked Kennedy.

"It's an organization that adopts dogs who are about to be euthanized if they aren't adopted. They get the dogs together and smuggle them out of state to a no-kill shelter."

"That's awesome. My parents' dog was rescued from a kill shelter. She's the best dog. She's very sweet. She's about ten years old now."

Kennedy was following Rosie with her eyes the whole time. Rosie could run laps around the other dogs at the dog park. She would pester the other dogs to make them chase her. Kennedy had to watch her to make sure she didn't make a larger dog so angry that they got into a fight.

She turned her attention back to the man on the bench. He was what her friends would call TDH—tall, dark, and handsome. He had dark black hair and dark black eyes with a well-trimmed beard and a healthy tan. He was maybe late twenties or early thirties. He was wearing a button-up fishing shirt, shorts, and Chaco's.

She realized she was pretty grungy at that moment. Her wavy hair was pulled back in a running headband. She had her torn-up jean shorts on, a tank top that illustrated all the mountains in Arkansas, and her Teva sandals, which she wore only to the dog park. To top it off, she had not put any makeup on that day. She decided that she was definitely keeping her sunglasses on.

"My name is Kennedy, by the way," she said.

"I'm Jason. Nice to meet you." He moved a little closer to where she was. "Have you climbed all the mountains on your shirt?"

"I hiked most of them when I was younger, yes. But I would by no means call it mountain climbing. The Ozarks are like dinosaur droppings compared to the Rockies and the Apps. I've climbed Pinnacle a couple of times since I've been in Little Rock, though."

"How long have you been here?"

"I moved here in January. So, almost eight months."

"That's longer than I've been here," he said. "I just got back this month."

"Where were you before this?"

"I was traveling around the United States on a year-long sabbatical. Before that, I lived in New Mexico for four years. My mom and my sister live here in Little Rock. I'm trying to decide what to do next with my life."

"What did you do when you worked in New Mexico?"

"I worked in computer sales. I made a lot of money working for HP. What do you do here in Little Rock?" asked Jason.

"I'm a dentist."

"What? You look so young! How old are you?"

"Twenty-seven."

"That's so young!"

"I can be a dentist and be twenty-seven. I graduated school when I was twenty-five," said Kennedy.

She wished sometimes she could tell people she was a nurse. For some reason, that seemed more reasonable to most people.

"You look really young to be a dentist."

"I hear that every day. You do know that ageism is discrimination as well…right?" she asked, smiling.

"Ha. Yeah, I guess it is. What book are you reading?" asked Jason, quickly changing the subject.

"It's called *The Last Chance Saloon*," replied Kennedy.

"I've never heard of it. What's it about?" said Jason.

"Well, it's about three women in their early thirties who are in their last-chance saloon," said Kennedy.

"What does that even mean?" asked Jason.

"These women are at the end of their dating prime, and they all fear ending up single forever. My mom gave it to me to read. She has a fear of me becoming a spinster. I'm five chapters in, and I've been reading it all summer. I'm not too motivated to finish it."

"That sounds really cheesy," said Jason.

Kennedy agreed.

After talking for a while, they realized they had both gone to the same college and knew a couple of the same people. Kennedy was three years younger than he was. Then Kennedy realized they had been talking for almost thirty minutes and that they were alone on the park bench. Jason's mom and sister were standing near the exit gate with the dogs on leashes. He stood up in front of her on the bench and said, "It looks like they're ready to leave. Do you think I could get your number and call you sometime?"

Year of Yes, thought Kennedy. She gave him her number. Then she went to catch Rosie before she got into a fight with the corgi guarding a Frisbee.

Jason called her the following Monday and asked her to go to dinner with him on Wednesday. They met at the Red Door Restaurant in Riverdale. Jason was waiting at a table for two. When Kennedy walked in, he pulled out a chair for her.

"Would you like some wine?" he asked.

"Definitely," said Kennedy.

"So, I didn't really know what to expect when you came in. I like your eyes. Why did you wear your sunglasses the entire time at the dog park?" asked Jason.

"I didn't have any makeup on, and the sun was out. Was I supposed to take them off?" asked Kennedy.

"Well, I didn't know what your eyes looked like. Also, I might have thought you were high at the dog park," said Jason.

"What? You thought I was high at the dog park? Ha! Well, I was wearing Tevas and ratty clothes. Rosie gets so muddy there, I can't wear regular clothes. So I guess that I was looking the part of a stoner," said Kennedy.

"Do you like Little Rock thus far?" asked Jason.

"It's been interesting. It's been a little difficult finding friends here who aren't married with children," said Kennedy.

"All of the friends that I have here are married with children. So I understand your problem. That's normal when you're in your late twenties and early thirties," said Jason.

"I also feel like the city is very divided into niches. For instance, the transplants hang out downtown, while the locals hang out in Hillcrest or the Heights. I kind of like the downtown urban area more than West Little Rock. But I live in Midtown, so I can get the best of all the areas. Also, there is West Little Rock, which is new, and everyone is shifting there."

"Yeah, that's called white flight," said Jason.

"What? I've never heard this. But that definitely sounds racist," said Kennedy.

"Oh, it is. Most of the crime here is black on black. The crime rates in Hillcrest and the Heights have risen in the last few years, and everyone is moving west. Plus, it's cheaper to live out there. New developments are always cheaper," said Jason.

"There is definitely white-on-white crime here too. You would think they would want to put more money into education and changing things in their neighborhoods than just running from it."

"Some parts of this city are built on decades of ignorance. This is where the Little Rock Nine happened, remember?"

"Yes, I remember hearing about that. Also, it seems like they're destroying a lot of beautiful land to sprawl out in the west. We call ourselves the Natural State, but Arkansans don't always seem to care about preserving nature."

"You are such a hippie. You're like a hippie with your shit together. It baffles me." Jason laughed.

BAGGAGE

On their second date, Jason took Kennedy to a Little Rock Travelers baseball game in North Little Rock. They had general seating tickets in the beer garden. They ate baseball-park food for dinner. Kennedy wore a white shirt and dribbled the mustard from her hot dog on it.

When ordering beer, Kennedy and Jason were in line behind one of her old friends, Mary. Mary and Kennedy had been church-camp counselors together. They hadn't seen each other in years. As soon as they recognized each other, they bear-hugged the way long-lost friends do.

"How's your brother doing?" asked Mary.

"He's good! He lives in Texas now with his wife," said Kennedy.

"I haven't seen him since he crashed my wedding to check out the venue for you. Did y'all end up getting married at the pavilion in the park where Mike and I did?" asked Mary.

Kennedy realized that Mary thought Jason was her husband. The last thing Mary had heard was that Kennedy was engaged. Kennedy glanced over at Jason, and he looked dumbfounded.

"No, actually, I didn't end up getting married," said Kennedy. "This is my date, Jason."

"Oh…" said Mary. "I didn't realize…umm…Hi, Jason. Nice to meet you. I think I should go back to my seat now! It was really good seeing you again, Kennedy."

"You too, Mary," said Kennedy.

Jason and Kennedy ordered their beers and walked all the way to the outfield to sit in the grass.

"So…you were engaged?" said Jason.

"Ha. Yes, I moved here after we broke up," said Kennedy.

"Why Little Rock?"

"It was the first place that offered a job. It was close enough to my family to be comfortable yet far enough away to still have a life. Little Rock was a soft place to land after a tough fall."

"Here's my dirty laundry: I just got out of a nine-year relationship. We broke up last month."

"Wow, I think you won!" said Kennedy. "I was in mine for four, and it's been eight months since we were together."

"At this age, I would expect you to have a little baggage. At least you don't have kids. You don't have kids, right?" asked Jason.

"Right. No kids." Kennedy laughed.

Kennedy realized that at this point, she was ready to start a new, committed relationship with someone. She had almost just jumped into one with David. But this guy most likely was not ready to get involved in a serious relationship. She was not going to pressure him into anything he wasn't ready for, either.

After talking all night and never actually watching the game, they looked up at the scoreboard and noticed that the Travelers had won. There was a fireworks show after the game, and Kennedy and Jason stayed to watch. Jason put his arm around Kennedy and leaned in for a long kiss.

"This may sound like it's out of the blue. But do you know how to drive a boat?" asked Kennedy.

"Yes, I can drive a boat. Why?"

"I have five friends coming into town next weekend. We've rented a house on Lake Hamilton in Hot Springs. It supposedly has an island, a fire pit, and a pontoon boat. None of us wants to be the responsible driver for the day. We need a driver," said Kennedy.

"Are these all girls?"

"Yes, they all went to dental school with me."

"So, six female dentists and me on a pontoon boat," said Jason.

"Yes. That is correct."

"I believe I can do that," he said with a smile.

CAPTAIN BLACKBEARD

The weather was getting cooler in Arkansas, and the humid days of summer were starting to wane. This was going to be a perfect girls' weekend. Kennedy and Bailey had been planning it for months. It had been Bailey's suggestion to go to Hot Springs to rent out a vacation home on Lake Hamilton. The vacation spot, called Paradise Island, had a boat dock, a pontoon, a paddle boat, a fire pit, and a sand volleyball court. Bailey and Kennedy surfed through dozens of rentals on the website Vacation Rental by Owner. They found one that had the perfect amenities and was inexpensive and plunked down money on it right away. They were so excited that they failed to read the part about the owner of this rental living upstairs with his wife. They had to break the news to all the girls before they collected money from them. Everybody agreed to make the best of the situation.

Kennedy spent the last Thursday night in August baking gluten-free, penis-shaped cupcakes in preparation for the bachelorette lake weekend. She also made non-gluten-free, penis-shaped chocolate cupcakes. When the cupcakes came out of the oven, she started laughing so hard that there were tears in her eyes. The chocolate ones came out much larger than the gluten-free vanilla ones. Kennedy made funny videos of the cupcakes and sent them to the girls.

She was excited for everyone to get there on Friday. Jenna was flying from New York. Kate and Zoe were flying in from Knoxville. Bailey was flying in from Atlanta. And Cassie, the recently engaged bachelorette, was driving up from Shreveport and bringing her dog, Peanut.

Kennedy took off work on Friday. She picked up Bailey, Kate, Jenna, and Zoe from the Bill and Hillary Clinton International Airport. They all loaded into the car and went to a lingerie store to buy Cassie necessary items for her bachelorette weekend. Then they loaded Rosie and Peanut up into their vehicles and headed to Lake Hamilton.

"Kennedy, it sounds like you're getting sick. You've almost lost your voice," said Zoe on the car ride there. Zoe, a stout brunette with large dark brown eyes and naturally tan skin, was always the mom of the group. She was the oldest in the group by five years. Zoe had worked in New York City as an intern for Vogue before going back to school for Dentistry. She could be sassy in three different languages (French, Spanish, and English). Also, she was never afraid to tell you want was on her mind.

"I know. I've been doing this whole Year of Yes thing. I've been out every night this week doing something. But on Wednesday, I smoked a large chocolate cigar and drank whiskey with our office manager and a new orthodontist they were recruiting for the practice. I think it was the cigar that gave me the sore throat," said Kennedy.

"Was the orthodontist cute?" asked Bailey.

"She was a woman. She was cute. But I prefer men." Kennedy laughed.

"You need to slow down, Kennedy, or you're going to wear yourself out," said Zoe.

"We will *not* be slowing down this weekend!" said Bailey, who was cuddled with Rosie in the backseat of the car.

"I'll be fine. I got this," said Kennedy, who had no plans of slowing down.

The first day at Paradise Island, the group made a trip to the grocery store to stock up on food and beer. Then the girls each grabbed a raft and floated the afternoon away in the water off of the dock in front of the rental house. Bob Marley and Ben Harper played loudly from a Bluetooth speaker as Peanut and Rosie in their doggie lifejackets swam around the girls on their rafts.

"How did Grant propose to you?" Kate asked Cassie.

"Yes! We want to hear the story!" said Bailey.

"Well, it was a busy morning at work. I was having a rough day because I was overbooked, and all of my patients seemed to have ridiculous problems. Then, right before lunch, my last patient was an add-on. On this patient's chart was the name Willuam Arryme. I joked with one of my technicians about how silly the name was. Then I knocked on the door, entered the room, and there was Grant. He was down on one knee with a ring in his hands. He said some really loving words, but blurted them out very quickly. I, of course, said yes."

"Oh my gosh! Will U Marry Me? That is so sweet and awesome!" said Kate, and all the other girls agreed.

The next day, the six women went to the Quapaw Hot Baths and Spa. They rotated through the different-temperature pools. Then they each got a deep-tissue massage and a facial. After that they went to dinner at an Italian restaurant down the street. On the way back to the car, the girls stopped at a gift shop. They all bought cheesy, matching Hot Springs tank tops to wear on their boating adventure the next day.

It started to rain heavily when they got back to the house. So they played Cards Against Humanity and the new Heads Up! game on their phones. They drank heavily and talked and laughed loudly. They never heard from their upstairs chaperones. It was one of the greatest rainy nights.

Jason showed up promptly at 10:30 a.m. Sunday to drive the boat.

"Welcome to Paradise Island," Kennedy told Jason. Then she introduced Jason to all of the girls as they were loading up the boat.

"I have a few friends that are out on the lake this weekend. Is it cool if we meet up with them?" asked Jason.

"Yeah, that sounds good. Do you know where they're going to be?" asked Kennedy.

"They told us to meet them at Party Cove," said Jason.

"Party Cove? I'm so ready for this!" said Bailey.

The girls all agreed. They finished loading up the boat. They left Rosie and Peanut back at the house and headed out on Lake Hamilton.

"I know the perfect song for this ride," said Meredith as she pulled up the song by Little Big Town on her Bluetooth speaker:

> *Floatin' is all I wanna do.*
> *You can climb the ladder,*
> *Just don't rock the boat while I barbeque*
> *On the pontoon.*

Party Cove was full of boats with people drinking and partying. Most of the people were regulars at Party Cove on Lake Hamilton. The girls pulled their boat up next to some of Jason's friends. There were two married couples. They had two small corgis onboard each wearing lifejackets. on.

The six long-lost friends got their rafts out and floated by the boat. They all had beers in their hands and were relaxed completely.

"I'm so glad you didn't marry Sam," Jenna told Kennedy. "I really liked him. He was a good guy. But I'm glad you didn't marry him."

"Thanks, Jenna. I think I'm happier now. You're right; he was a good guy. I don't think, in the end, he was my guy," said Kennedy.

"Yeah, Kennedy. Now you're living the life in Party Cove with that hottie driving our boat. What's his name again?" asked Kate.

"His name is Jason. He kind of looks like Jon Hamm, right? I love Jon Hamm," said Kennedy, smiling as she took a drink of her beer.

"I think I'm going to call him Blackbeard. Because he has a black beard and he's driving our boat," said Kate.

"Captain Blackbeard!" said Bailey, who was thoroughly intoxicated at this point.

"Have you slept with him yet?" asked Kate.

"No. We've only kissed a couple of times," replied Kate.

"That's probably why he's driving the boat for us," said Bailey.

Kennedy swam back to the boat to see what Blackbeard was up to. She saw that he was talking to his friends on the party barge. She jumped onto the neighboring boat, a much nicer boat than their little pontoon, and tapped Jason on the back.

"Are you smoking a cigarette?" asked Kennedy.

"Does it look like I am? Do you want a hit?" said Jason.

"No," said Kennedy. *Yes to smoking a cigarette.* Then she took the cigarette out of his hand and took a long drag.

"I didn't know you smoked," said Kennedy.

"I didn't know you did either," replied Jason.

"I don't. I hate smoking. It just felt right."

Then the group heard screaming coming from the water. It was Bailey. She had been swimming with the corgis in the water. One of the corgis had bitten her on the cheek. The owner of the offending corgi happened to be a primary care physician in Hot Springs. He apologized to Bailey as he pulled her into the boat to take a look at the damage.

"It looks like a small scratch on your cheek," said the doctor. He pulled some Neosporin and Band-Aids out of a first-aid kit. "It should be fine soon. Please don't have my dog put down," he joked.

The rest of the day in Party Cove was slightly hazy for the six drunken dentists. Bailey and the doctor ended up making up. She completely forgot about being bitten by the corgi. The girls danced and laughed so hard that their cheeks hurt.

Jason drove them back to the rental house a little later than expected. The sun was setting, and the man who owned the boat had called several times. No one was worried. They made it back right as the sun was slipping into the darkness.

The next day, the women returned to their respective states. They made a pact to do a girls' trip every Labor Day weekend. The pact wasn't kept. But they all managed to keep up with one another through emails, texts and an occasional dental conferences.

9. SEPTEMBER

September, I'll remember
A love once new has grown old.

—Simon and Garfunkel

CRINKLE FRY

Kennedy was sick for a week after the Labor Day trip. She had a severe upper respiratory infection. She had to cancel two of her clinic days seeing patients. She tried to never take sick days and to take only vacation days. However, Kennedy had worn herself out completely. This Year of Yes was taking a toll on her immune system.

When she was feeling better, Jason invited her to dinner and drinks that Friday. He picked her up at her townhouse and took her out to eat at a restaurant called the Pantry. When it came time to pay the check, Kennedy offered to pay. She knew he didn't have a job. They had just talked about it over dinner. He hadn't had a job in over a year. He had just been driving around the country going on adventures, which was an awesome thing to do. However, Kennedy figured that by the end of an adventure like that, he might be out of money.

"I got this," said Jason. "Don't worry about it."

He took her out to dinner again on Saturday night. At the end of every night out, he would always walk her to her door like a gentleman. They would make out. Then he would leave.

While out with the girls Monday night, Kennedy asked her friends about Jason or Blackbeard, as they referred to him. Kennedy, Robyn, Micah, and Sarah had been watching *The Bachelor* together on Monday nights since Andy's season of *The Bachelorette* had started at the beginning of Kennedy's Year of Yes. Before that year, Kennedy had not liked *The Bachelor*. But it was the Year of Yes, and she needed girlfriends in her new city. By this time in September, they were watching *Bachelor in Paradise* - which was even cheesier than all the Bachelor/Bachelorette shows. However, Kennedy was hooked.

"I'm very confused about the guy I've been dating—you know, Jason," said Kennedy.

"The guy you met at the dog park? How so?" asked Micah.

"He keeps taking me out to nice places and paying for everything. But he doesn't have a job," said Kennedy.

"Maybe he's a trust-fund baby," said Sarah.

"He's could be a drug dealer. Didn't he think you were high when you met him?" asked Micah.

"Maybe he's intimidated by you and your success. So he still wants to be the man and pay for things," said Robyn.

"These are all feasible options. Although I'm not that successful yet," said Kennedy. "The other weird thing is we haven't done anything more than kiss. He doesn't seem like he's in a hurry, either," said Kennedy.

"He's probably just old fashioned," said Sarah.

"That's not a thing," said Micah. "I think he's scared. He's just intimidated by you and your independent personality."

"Maybe he's just not that into me," said Kennedy.

"No way. He wouldn't be buying you dinner with his drug money if he wasn't that into you," said Micah.

"I really hope he's not a drug dealer." Kennedy laughed.

⊷ ⊶

On Wednesday of that week, Jason invited Kennedy to dinner again. It was their fifth date. This time they ate at Capers, which was an even more expensive restaurant in Little Rock. After driving back from dinner, Kennedy invited Jason in for a drink. She was determined to take this relationship to the next level.

They were on the couch and Kennedy had consumed half of her beer while talking when Jason leaned in to give her a kiss. They started kissing intensely. Jason tugged her hips gently guided her on top of him to straddle his legs. The kissing continued. Then Jason pulled off her shirt. Kennedy started unbuttoning his shirt. Jason unsnapped her bra and kissed her breasts. Kennedy reached down to undo the button and zipper of his pants. Jason was breathing heavily—very heavily.

Suddenly, Kennedy realized that Jason was also sweating heavily—too heavily. She did not feel anything under his pants. Jason's eyes glazed over, and his face turned pale as sweat rolled down his face. They stopped making out. Kennedy realized what was happening: he was having a vasovagal response. Kennedy saw three patients have vasovagal responses when they were getting their teeth examined in dental school.

"Are you okay?" asked Kennedy as she climbed off of him and began putting her clothes back on.

"Yes, I'm fine," said Jason quietly.

"It doesn't look like you're okay. We should probably cool it," said Kennedy. "Do you want a glass of water? Sometimes it helps to put your head in between your legs."

"Water will be fine," said Jason, still sweating and breathing heavy.

Kennedy went to the kitchen to pour a glass of water and grab a towel. Jason put his shirt back on and put his head between his legs. Sweat continued to drip profusely off of his face.

"Has this happened before?" asked Kennedy.

"Only once, in college," said Jason. He was embarrassed. "It was with a girl I dated before my ex-girlfriend. She told all of her friends after it happened."

He paused and said, "I think you're just too thin for me."

"What? I'm not that thin," said Kennedy. She hadn't seen that coming. Then she realized how embarrassed Jason actually was.

"My ex-girlfriend was larger than you. It's just not the same," said Jason.

"Well, that doesn't make it any better," said Kennedy, rolling her eyes.

"Did you think that we were going to have sex tonight?" said Jason. "We've only been on like five dates. Isn't it a little soon? Is sex all you care about?"

"Whoa! First of all, I definitely think five dates is a long enough time before you have sex. We're adults. It's part of the relationship and getting to know each other. Second of all, you had a vasovagal response and couldn't get an erection. Now you're just being a jerk," said Kennedy.

"Whatever. Maybe you're just a slut," said Jason.

"Yeah, that's not it," said Kennedy, now fuming. She knew he was embarrassed but blaming her was going too far. "You need to leave right now," she said, and she pointed to the door.

On Jason's way out, Rosie jumped up and bit the tail end of his shirt, tearing a chunk of fabric out of it. Kennedy couldn't help but laugh out loud. Not surprisingly, she never saw Jason/Blackbeard again.

PUBLIC SPEAKING

The next day was Thursday. A pre-health professions club at the University of Arkansas, Fayetteville had invited Kennedy was to give a presentation about dentistry. The drive from Little Rock to Fayetteville gave her time to replay the previous night and determine if she was at fault in any way. No, she decided. She brushed Blackbeard off as a loss and focused on what was ahead.

Kennedy wasn't the best when it came to public speaking. In fact, in school, she had actively avoided raising her hand and asking questions so as not to embarrass herself. When she did raise her hand to talk, she did, in fact, embarrass herself. But she said yes to the invitation.

Kennedy took the afternoon off and drove up through the Ozark Mountains to the University of Arkansas. She arrived earlier than expected. She drove around the campus and landed at Wilson Park. Kennedy got out of the car and sat down at a table under the pavilion in the park. It was a small park that was walking distance to campus. It had tennis courts, a large playground, and a pool that would show dive-in movies on hot summer weekends.

Kennedy was making notes for her presentation about career choices when it started to pour down buckets of rain out of nowhere. She stopped and looked around the park. It was completely empty, and she was alone. The memories from her college days here came flooding back. She remembered walking with friends under the towering sycamore and oak trees, having sorority/fraternity mud wars, and having outdoor zoology class there. In college for spending money, she babysat for several families in town and would take the kids here in the summers. She had had her first big heart break in this park. There was a loud clap of thunder and Kennedy shivered as she realized that her past was dancing all around her.

Kennedy was one of the last speakers to give a presentation. It looked as if she was the youngest of all the health professionals. She sat through the optometrist, the physical therapist, the pharmacist, and the physician's assistant. When it was Kennedy's turn, she took the microphone and could feel her hands shaking.

"Hi. My name is Kennedy James. I'm a dentist in Little Rock. I graduated five years ago from the University of Arkansas. Actually, my first class ever as a freshman was held in this auditorium. I remember my first day of class being very scary. I was thinking how enormous this auditorium was, and it was full of strangers. For some reason, today it looks a lot smaller and less overwhelming." Kennedy paused to take a sip of water and spilt a little down her chin and on her shirt. She wiped her chin with her hand, composed herself, and continued.

"How many of you here are considering dentistry as a career?" asked Kennedy.

Out of the 120 students in the auditorium, ten hands went up.

"Tough crowd," said Kennedy, and a couple of people laughed. "First, let me tell you a little bit about a career in dentistry. It's a four-year degree after college…"

After the presentations were over, a gaggle of students got up to ask the speakers questions. Most of them were there to talk to the physician's assistant. With the recent shift toward primary care, that job was in high demand. It was just close enough to being a doctor and many students believed it was a much easier degree to obtain than other medical fields.

One of the girls there had just been accepted to dental school and wanted to talk to Kennedy. Kennedy shared notes about school with her. She told her where to live and how it was best to choose a roommate who was in school with you. Kennedy hoped she had made a difference somehow by giving this speech. She felt more confident that she could speak again in public.

BIRTHDAY WISHES

"Happy Birthday Sporty Spice," said David over facetime.

"You know I hate that nickname. It's offensive to my little boobs," replied Kennedy.

"I like your boobs. Also, Sporty Spice was my favorite. You are looking very cute on your birthday. How old are you again? Twenty-six?"

"Yup. You got it!" Kennedy smiled. She didn't feel twenty-eight and she wasn't about to admit it.

"How was your birthday?"

"It was good. At work we ate a cake shaped like a mouth full of teeth. I drank two glasses of wine at happy hour with Robin and Micah. Then, I picked up a

FaceTime from a guy who I haven't heard from since he couldn't make it to Little Rock."

"I know. To be fair, Kennedy, you told me you didn't feel like talking to me for a while. Then you ignored a bunch of my late night drunk text messages."

"You're right. At the time it seemed that your car was more important to you than me."

Would this man always frustrate and excite her at the same time, thought Kennedy.

"I'm sorry about that. Kennedy, I don't think I'm ready to come back to Little Rock just yet. There is so much more to explore out here. Also, I'll be busy with my new flight training program. But, you should come visit me."

"David, one sided long distance relationships never work. I don't want to be the one flying back and forth. But, thank you for the birthday wishes," said Kennedy, getting so frustrated that she couldn't make eye contact through the camera with him.

"Well, I think you're a great gal. Tell Rosie I say hi. I'll still be here for you. Call me any time you want to talk."

I need a lover that won't drive me crazy
I need a lover that won't drive me crazy
I need a lover that won't drive me crazy

- John Mellencamp

THE NONALCOHOLIC

The second Thursday in September, Rosie started puppy-training classes. Rosie was already a fast learner. However, Kennedy needed her to be a little better behaved and listen to her commands.

There was only one other person in the class—a man who looked to be around Kennedy's age. His name was Kurt, and he was there with his dog, Fido. Fido, a border collie mix was about two months younger than Rosie. The two puppies played together as soon as they saw each other. Kurt was maybe only a few inches taller than Kennedy. He was slim, muscular, with sandy brown hair large green eyes and a lopsided grin. He was a real-estate broker who had grown up in Little Rock.

Kennedy realized she would be spending the next four weeks in puppy-training class with this guy. She hoped he didn't have a girlfriend.

Kurt and she talked after class. He invited her to Señor Tequila to watch one of his friends play in his band.

"I'm sorry; I already have plans with some friends. I think we're going to Cajun's, if you want to come," said Kennedy.

"I told my friend that I would come to his show. But maybe next time," said Kurt.

"What a cute way to meet a guy!" said Robyn later that night at Cajun's. "When you live happily ever after, you can tell people that you met at puppy-training class."

"Every way is a cute way to meet," said Kennedy. "I'm so tired of meeting guys. I think I'm ready for something serious. I don't want to just keep meeting guys. If my life were a movie, it would all be meet cutes without a happy ending. I want to be in a comfortable relationship already," said Kennedy.

"Comfortable? Tyler and I have comfortable. It's so boring. I live vicariously through you and your endearing singleness!" said Robyn.

"Well, the grass is always greener on the other side," Kennedy retorted.

The next Thursday, after puppy-training class, Kurt asked her to go to Señor Tequila again. This time

Kennedy said yes. She took Rosie home and met Kurt at the restaurant.

Kurt was there with his dad and two of his dad's friends. Kennedy thought this was a little strange and too soon to be meeting a parent. She scanned the table. None of them were drinking alcohol. It was all water or soda. She was on call that night and hadn't planned on drinking. But now she had the urge to drink.

"I'll have a Diet Coke. I'm on call this week, so I won't have a beer," said Kennedy.

"Oh, none of us drink alcohol," said Kurt.

"Oh, I didn't realize," said Kennedy.

This was shocking to Kennedy. It was strange because this guy looked as if he partied a lot. Maybe it was just a front he put on for his dad?

"Do you go to church anywhere here, Kennedy?" asked Kurt's dad.

"I've gone to Holy Souls a couple of times, and I go to church when I go home," said Kennedy.

"Oh, you're Catholic?" said Kurt's dad, shooting a quizzical look toward Kurt.

"Yes, I identify myself as Catholic. I don't make it to church as often as I should," said Kennedy.

"You should have Kurt take you to our church, First Christian in Maumelle. He plays the guitar for the youth choir. He's very good," said Kurt's dad.

"That sounds cool. I think I'm probably just going to stay a cafeteria Catholic for now. I'll think about it, though." Kennedy smiled, not wanting to be too rude. She respected that they had a strong church community. However, she had no interest in an organization that didn't drink alcohol.

After the band's set was over, Kurt walked her to her car. He told her he had a lot of fun and asked her to hang out that weekend with her. Kennedy told him maybe and that she might be out of town. When he called the next day, she told him that she was going to her parents' for the weekend and that she would see him the next Thursday. She had no real plans to go and ended up staying in town. She didn't want to lead him on; he seemed like a sweet guy.

10. OCTOBER

I know how to stand there
Still till the moon rise up
Right behind the pine,
Oh, Lord, October road.

—James Taylor

MYSTERY SOLVED

By fall, Kennedy had become a regular at Town Pump on Tuesday night karaoke night. She would go at least once a month to sing. Micah and some other friends would also join. The bartenders all knew her by name. This particular Tuesday, the last Tuesday in September, Kennedy met her Snapchat stalker.

She sang "Rumor Has It" by Adele. As soon as she left the stage, Kennedy got a Snapchat. It was a picture of her singing onstage. On top of the photo were the words "Are you here tonight?" Kennedy hurried to the bar to show Micah the snap, but it was gone before she got there.

"My Snapchat stalker is here somewhere," Kennedy told Micah.

"Kennedy, do you know how ridiculous that sounds?" said Micah.

Kennedy looked around and found Sarah, Drew, and Steve. Steve was making eye contact with her. Then he held up his phone and smiled at her. Kennedy walked to the other side of the bar.

"Are you my creepy Snapchat stalker?" asked Kennedy.

"Yes, I thought you would figure this out by now," said Steve.

"Umm…I looked up your screen name and got a Twitter account for a Steven in Detroit who looked nothing like you. I don't remember exchanging Snapchat names with you," said Kennedy.

"We definitely exchanged Snapchat names. We were drunk, and you told me that you were an awesome Snapchatter. I never got a snap from you. Then I saw you on the plane. I really did see you on the plane. You just didn't remember that we had exchanged Snapchat names and you freaked out," said Steve.

"Well I'm happy that you're not a real stalker. But you could have answered the snap back," said Kennedy.

"Yeah, I thought it would be funnier if you didn't know who it was," said Steve.

"Great way to be creepy."

"By the way, you're getting pretty good at Karaoke."

Kennedy blushed, "Thanks, I've been working on it."

GUIDELINES TO BEING A KARAOKE QUEEN

By Kennedy Michelle James

1. Never apologize for being too pitchy. No one cares. They are all drunk.
2. Never drop the mic after (what you think is) an amazingly moving and utterly brilliant performance. The microphones cost a lot of money. If you break it, you might have to replace it.
3. Never get up on stage and sing while another person is singing. Especially if it's another karaoke queen. You might get murdered or at least be shoved off the stage and maybe break a leg.

4. Blacking out and drunk dancing on the stage while other people sing is only okay for a little bit and only if you dance for the right person. The friendly bouncer may or may not escort you to a cab. (That one is for Bailey.)

5. If you're going to sing a slow song or ballad, dedicate it to someone before you start singing. That way the audience realizes there is a reason why you're putting them through so much misery.
   a. "This song goes out to my dog that died."
      i. Cue "I Will Always Love You," Whitney Houston.
   b. "This song goes out to…"

6. Karaoke DJs can be complete assholes. Always be kind to them. They've spent most of their lives waiting for their big musical break. Now they are catering to drunken wannabes who slobber all over their expensive equipment.

7. If you tip the DJ, sometimes he or she will move your song up a couple of slots in line. This helps when you want to tab out and go to the next bar. Or when you are singing karaoke on a work night and need to get home before midnight.
   a. Sometimes you think the karaoke DJ is being a bitch by skipping you or putting other people in front of you. But, in reality, the other people tipped. Because the other people wanted to go home or to the next bar.

8. Never go to karaoke alone. Always have backup. Find a couple of friends who appreciate karaoke as much as you do. Even if they don't sing.

9. Never be embarrassed to sing whatever you want. If it's horrible, you can still own it.

10. Never take karaoke too seriously. For some people it's a rush that gets them out of their comfort zone. For others, it's a chance to show off their mediocre or surprisingly amazing singing voice. Either way, embrace this moment. Because for this one short moment in time, you own that stage. You belong there. No matter how much weight you gained recently or how horrible your day has been or what your boyfriend/mom/boss just said to you. This is your moment. You can be whoever you want to be and sing however you want to sing. Nothing else matters at this moment. In this one particular moment in time, you are the karaoke queen.

Side note: I am completely aware of my addiction to karaoke. At least it's not opioids.

THE KNEELER

Little Rocktoberfest was always the first weekend in October at War Memorial Stadium and it was always a big deal. Kennedy, Robyn, Sarah, and Micah walked from Micah's house in Hillcrest to the stadium. They waited in a long line to sample beers from a number of local restaurants and breweries. There were several people there whom Kennedy knew, including some of her patients. She felt as if Little Rock was getting smaller and smaller.

The group tasted different beers. There were so many types of pumpkin ales. Kennedy's favorite was the Loblolly pumpkin ale ice cream. Beer and ice cream were two of her favorite things.

Kennedy, Robyn, Sarah, and Micah were standing in a group when Robyn noticed a very tall, skinny man kneeling on one knee.

"Look, is that guy going to propose?" asked Robin.

"He's standing next to a guy, but I won't rule anything out," said Sarah.

The group kept talking, and the man kept kneeling. Kennedy looked at him, and they made eye contact. She thought she knew him from somewhere. She couldn't put her finger on it.

A few hours later, the girls were thoroughly drunk and full as they walked back to Micah's house. Kennedy checked her phone; she had a message on Facebook. It was from a guy named Sam Howell, whom she was apparently already friends with. She didn't remember who he was.

Sam Howell: Hey! I just saw you at Little Rocktoberfest. Do you live here now?

Kennedy: I'm sorry. How do I know you?

Kennedy scrolled through his Facebook photos quickly.

Kennedy: Wait. Were you just kneeling at War Memorial Stadium?

Sam Howell: Yes, that was me. Ha ha.

"Ask him why he was kneeling!" said Micah after Kennedy told her who the guy was.

"It was so weird," said Robyn.

Kennedy: Why were you kneeling?

Sam Howell: I rode in a seventy-five-mile bike race this morning, and my legs were giving out. Also, we went to college together. That's why we're already friends on Facebook.

Kennedy: Oh. I'm sorry I don't remember you that well. Yes, I do live here now.

Sam: That's cool. We should hang out sometime. Can I have your number?

Kennedy: Sure—555-236-1875.

Sam Howell: :-) Thanks!

"He asked for my number, and I gave it to him," Kennedy told the girls.

"That's good! I think? It was still strange that he was kneeling," said Micah.

"He has the same name as my ex-fiancé. I think I'm going to start calling him by his last name—Howell. His name is Howell now," said Kennedy.

"I'm just going to refer to him as the Kneeler," said Robyn.

MEMORY LANE

Kennedy was excited about going out with Sam Howell. They went on several dates and started seeing each other regularly. Sam Howell had gone to the same undergraduate school at U of A at the same time. So they had a lot to talk about. He was tall – even kneeling he was only a few inches shorter than Kennedy. His dark brown thick hair was tussled like he always just crawled out of bed. He had a sharp angular chin and a killer smile – beautiful perfectly white teeth. He was Methodist had a steady job as a manufacturing engineer. Also, he lived in Little Rock and was not planning on moving anywhere anytime soon. He definitely had potential.

"I'm going to be honest," said the Kneeler, mid-make-out session. "I had a huge crush on you in college."

Kennedy raised an eyebrow. She didn't remember him at all in college.

"Really? When did we hang out?" asked Kennedy.

"Well, I saw you at the library all the time," said the Kneeler.

"Ah, I practically lived at the library," said Kennedy.

"Also, I dated Piper for a little bit. But she threw me to the curb and started dating a Sigma Nu."

"Oh? You used to date Piper? I'm sorry to tell you, but I don't remember that either."

"Yeah, it was the beginning of junior year. I drove you and Piper back to her place from a party once. I think the party was at your house, actually. I went to some of the parties at your house. Do you remember one that the cops busted?"

"Oh my gosh! How do you remember this? Those are such blurry college days. The cops definitely busted that party. I must have been so upset that I didn't realize who took me to Piper's. Also, I met so many people at those parties," said Kennedy.

"Your roommates were definitely on drugs," said the Kneeler.

"I think they were just smoking weed and drinking. I'm not sure that they did anything harder than that. Either way, I was way soberer than they were. That house was drama. Wait, you were the one who told me that my roommates were white trash!" said Kennedy.

"Yeah, I don't remember that," said Howell.

"You drove Piper and me back to Piper's apartment that night of the party. You told me, 'Don't worry about those girls. They're only white trash.'" Kennedy's eyes lit up. She was having an epiphany.

"That sounds like something I would say," said Howell.

"I went back to the house the next day. The girls cornered me again and cussed me out. To this day, I'm still uncertain what it was for. I think it was because at that party I was sober and laughing. They thought I hadn't taken the cop situation seriously. Anyways, I called them white trash after they yelled at me again. Of course, that made them even angrier. I'm certain that you're the reason why I called them white trash," said Kennedy.

"I didn't realize. I'm sorry. Did you end up making up with the girls?"

"No. It got even more complicated. During the party someone crawled up into the attic to avoid the police. He broke the air conditioner. Because the cops broke up a party and we had a broken air conditioner, we got an eviction notice from the company that owned the house," said Kennedy.

"Y'all were evicted?"

"I wish we had been evicted. One of the girls I lived with had her dad talk to the management. He paid to have the air conditioner fixed so that we could stay in the house," said Kennedy.

"So you stayed there?"

"No, the other girls did. But I got out of there. I moved in with Piper shortly after. Those girls never got over me calling them white trash."

"Girls have so much drama," said Howell.

"Yeah, we were young and drunk. Also, I think that you should have no more than two female roommates living under one roof. Someone always gets picked on or left out."

SAME NAME,
BUT DIFFERENT

K ennedy hung up the phone. Her friend Rachel
from North Carolina had just called. Rachel had
told Kennedy that she had just run into Sam and his
new girlfriend. Her name was Kennedy, and she was a
thin brunette in her early twenties. The two were at a
dental conference at the Grove Park Inn in Asheville.

Kennedy shuddered at this thought. At this time last
year, she and Sam had been staying at the Grove Park
Inn for the same conference. The year before, he had
proposed there.

Rachel said that Sam's girlfriend seemed nice and added, "But you're way cuter!"

Kennedy half suspected that Rachel was just being nice.

This was weird. Sam had replaced her with a girl who looked like her and had the same name. To top it off, he was taking her to the Grove Park Inn. Shivers went down her spine. She thought back to the week she had told Sam she was leaving.

He'd kept saying, "How do you think I feel? My fiancée is leaving me!" He'd said it multiple times. "*My* fiancée is leaving *me*."

This statement had made Kennedy want to leave even more. All she was to him was his fiancée. He thought he owned her. It was all about him. His family. His career. His things—and she was only one of them. She had lost so much of herself. She didn't want to be just his arm candy. His trophy wife.

She knew she didn't love him anymore. But his new girlfriend has the same name and he took her to the same hotel as she and Sam had visited a year ago? This felt strange. How could she be so replaceable? What if Sam gave the new Kennedy the same engagement ring he had given her?

She called her friend Sydney.

"You shouldn't be freaking out like this. You're dating a guy named Sam right now. Remember?" Sydney said over the phone.

"I know, but Sam is a common name. Kennedy is not. I don't know anyone else named Kennedy. Also, I call my Sam, Howell."

"I guess I see your point. What do you think she does for a living?"

Kennedy replied, "I'm not sure, but he couldn't handle the fact that I was in the same profession. He didn't want me to be a colleague of his. I can't imagine him ever dating another woman who is in the same field."

Sydney said, "Let's see what her Facebook page says."

They found out that the new Kennedy was an art instructor at a paint shop where mostly women gathered to drink wine and paint. She was a petite with large gray eyes—very similar to Kennedy's.

Kennedy had been to a painting class there with Rachel right several weeks before she moved away. She didn't remember another girl named Kennedy, though she did remember asking Sam to go there with her. He had turned her down right away and said she would have to go by herself. He had mentioned that it was too girly for him.

"Do you miss him ever?" asked Sydney.

"No. Actually, I think about him sometimes. I remember the fun things we did together and the friendship we had. But lately I keep thinking of this one fight that we had that was completely indicative of why our relationship ended."

"Oh, yeah? What was the fight about?" asked Sydney.

"We had taken a last-minute beach trip to Hilton Head with another couple from dental school. I realized two days into the trip that I had forgotten to pack underwear. We were in bathing suits the first couple of days. I didn't want the panty line from my bikini bottoms to show when we went to the restaurants and bars. Regardless, I shouldn't be defending myself. I needed underwear.

"Anyways, I asked Sam to go with me to buy some underwear at Target. It was about twenty-five minutes away from the beach house we were staying at. He grumbled but agreed to go with me. On the way to Target, we passed a Walgreens. He suggested we pull into Walgreens to find some underwear. Because he didn't want to go all the way to Target. He couldn't stand being away from the beach house this long. He never wanted to miss anything. So I pulled the car into Walgreens. As you can imagine, there was a limited selection of women's underwear at Walgreens. Lo and behold, there was one package of Hanes Her Way, size XL, full coverage, at this Walgreens."

"Did you go to Target?" asked Sydney.

"Yes, but before we did, he tried to convince me that I would be okay wearing the Hanes Her Way *extra-large* full-coverage underwear at the beach under my sundress."

"No he didn't!" said Sydney, laughing hysterically.

"I am a size small. I wear thongs. Here he was, trying to tell me that I would be fine wearing underwear three sizes too large for me. This was all because he wanted to get back to the beach house and not go to Target. I should have not invited him in the first place."

"That's ridiculous," said Sydney, still laughing.

"He bitched about it all the way to Target, too. He thought that I would be okay with whatever he gave me and just settle for things. He would not be okay wearing oversized boxer briefs under his pants. Why would I?"

And if you wanna keep me, then you better treat me
Like a damn princess, make that an empress
'Cause I'm so done, not being your number one
This superficial love

-Ruth B

11. NOVEMBER

My heart is dancin' to a November tune,
And I hope that you hear it singing songs
about you.
I sing songs of sorrow because you're
not around
See, babe, I'm gone tomorrow; baby,
follow me down.

—*The Avett Brothers*

FIRST PROPOSAL

After Kennedy's conversations with Rachel and Sydney about Sam dating another Kennedy, the memories came flooding back. Kennedy needed something to clear her head. She remembered Adrian's suggestion that she write about her time with Sam and her break up. So she picked up where she had left off, months ago and starting writing.

November was the month that Sam proposed. We were both in our last year of dental school. Sam and I were both on dental rotations in the Appalachian Mountains. We had chosen all of our rotations together and in North Carolina.

Sam told me to meet him at the Grove Park Inn after work on Friday. He told me that his cousin and his wife were going to meet us there for dinner. When I pulled up to the Grove Park Inn, I had the car valeted because I thought I was late and I knew Sam hated that. I texted Sam and told him that I was walking in the door. I asked him which restaurant he was in. Sam replied to stay there and that he would come and get me.

I waited in the Grand Hall of the Grove Park Inn for fifteen minutes before Sam showed up. He was wearing a brown suit and the blue tie I had bought him for his birthday. He was sweating and looked as if he had been running. In his hand was a disheveled rose.

"I didn't expect you to be here this early," said Sam. "Here, this is for you." He handed me the tattered drooping rose.

"Thank you for the rose. Where are your cousins?" I asked.

"We're going to meet them in their hotel room," he said. "Follow me."

Sam grabbed my hand and took me through the grand hall. We passed the gift shop, pictures of the presidents who had visited the giant hotel, and two large restaurants. He led me to a small corridor and then to an elevator that took us down three stories. His palms were sweating and pulsating as we rode the elevator in silence. I had a sense of what was about to happen. When the elevator doors opened, there was a trail of rose petals leading around the corner. This was it. The gears in my mind were turning.

We followed the trail of roses to a hotel-room door. Sam took out a room key and opened the door for me. The room was covered in rose petals. He held my hand and walked me into the room. Then he took the ring box from his pocket and bent down on one knee.

"Kennedy Michelle James, will you marry me?" asked Sam. He shook as if he were going to tumble over at any moment.

"Of course I will," I said. We kissed and hugged. Then we called everyone we knew to tell them the news.

I didn't cry. Should I have cried?

Kocaine Karolina down your bones
Fireworks in your heart make it far from home
Every morning you wake up alone just the same
Who would want to live longer anyway?

—*Elle King*

THE BANJO PLAYER

The second weekend in November, Robyn and Kennedy went to Afterthought in Hillcrest to see a local folk band. Kennedy had seen on Facebook that they were playing and she loved folk music.

"Where's the Kneeler?" asked Robyn as they shared a basket of Parmesan fries.

"It's hunting season. He's hunting. I don't know if I'm going see him anymore," replied Kennedy.

"Because it's hunting season? I never see Tyler during hunting season. With us being long distance, I probably go a month and a half without seeing him."

"I really don't know how you do that. You are stronger than me. But I don't think we're going to date anymore at all," said Kennedy.

"Oh, why not?" asked Robyn.

"I found out that he smokes cigarettes," said Kennedy. "I thought it wasn't a deal breaker—the cigarettes. I was just going to brush it off. But, hello, I'm a dentist. Why would I want to go out with someone that knowingly signs up for bad breath, yellow teeth and puts himself at risk for Leukoplakia or oral cancer? Plus, every time we kiss, I feel like I've smoked a pack of cigarettes. Sometimes I can smell it in his hair. It makes me gag. At this point, I think I'm just dating him because he's tall. I feel like our relationship has peaked."

"I'm sorry, Kennedy. I didn't think he was that special either. I never could carry a conversation with him."

"Me either. Also, he asked me to buy him a watch for Christmas."

"He wants your money."

"So does the institution! I'm drowning in student loans. I'm not buying him a watch," said Kennedy.

"That banjo player on stage is cute. Also, he keeps looking over here."

"Oh, yeah, I think I know him. He volunteered on the Better Block Project that I did this summer," said Kennedy. He did keep looking over in her direction. But she couldn't tell whether he was looking at her or the two girls at the table in front of them.

During intermission, the banjo player came over to the table and introduced himself. "Hi, I'm John Bellis. Weren't you on the Better Block Project with me?"

"Yes, you were the one who ran the rock wall," said Kennedy.

"Yeah, I help out the guy who owns it as a part-time job," said John.

"That's cool. Your band sounds great!" said Robyn.

"Thank you! Hey, I'm going to go grab a drink. But you two should stay after and have a drink with us," said John.

"That sounds good," said Kennedy.

John Bellis was a good-looking guy in his mid-twenties with a very nicely groomed beard. He had a Jake Gyllenhaal look about him with dark hair and large cobalt blue eyes. Also, he was short. In fact, at five seven, he was the same height as she.

It was twelve thirty in the morning when Robyn started getting restless. "I don't want to stay for the whole set. I'm getting tired. I'm too old for this!" she complained.

Kennedy was getting tired too. Also, she didn't want to sit and watch the band alone. So they agreed to leave.

Kennedy and Robyn paid their tabs and got up to walk out. As they walked out, Robyn saw John's big blue eyes follow Kennedy out the door. "You're leaving?" he mouthed to the girls as he continued to play the banjo and they walked out the door.

Robyn stopped Kennedy outside the bar. "That guy was definitely upset that you left," she said.

"Well, maybe we'll run into each other again. I'm tired too. I can't imagine what time they stop playing and how late they're staying out," said Kennedy.

⊷ ⊶

Each month on Tuesday, Kennedy volunteered for a dental clinic that extracted teeth at a Methodist church in Little Rock. Kennedy had started volunteering there in May as part of the Year of Yes. All of the patients were uninsured or couldn't afford regular dental appointments. Most of them were in pain from rotting teeth. A lot of them were Hispanic. This gave Kennedy great practice in brushing up on her clinical Spanish. She enjoyed doing the work. But however rewarding it was, it was exhausting. She only volunteered once a month.

This particular Tuesday, Kennedy ran into the banjo player again. He was unloading his truck in the church parking lot when Kennedy pulled up next to him. She was wearing her white coat scrubs, ready to see patients.

"Well, hello, Doctor!" said the banjo player as Kennedy got out of the car.

"Hey, I think I know you. What are you doing here?" asked Kennedy.

"My grandfather built this church. Unfortunately, that means that my family is charge of a lot of things, such as decorations. I brought some things to decorate the church for fall," said the banjo player.

"Wow, that's pretty cool. I didn't realize what a small community this was," said Kennedy.

"Why did you leave my show early on Saturday? I really wanted to hang out with you."

"Robyn, my friend—she really wanted to go to bed. She was tired. I have no better excuse. What time did you guys play till?"

"About two in the morning. Then we closed down the bar, went back to my house, and drank some more."

"Yeah, Robyn definitely wouldn't have stayed out that late. I don't know how you guys do that."

"It's only on nights that we have a show," said John.

"Well, I need to go see if I have a patient ready."

"Hey, do you want to go get drinks with me this weekend?"

"I'm going out of town this weekend."

"What about Wednesday?"

"Tomorrow? I can make that work," Kennedy replied.

The next day came too quickly for Kennedy. After packing for her trip to Denver, she met John at Bar Louie for drinks. She walked into the restaurant, and he was already sitting at a table. Kennedy sat across from him at the square table. He moved to sit next to her instead of across from her. He seemed very excited to hang out with her. Kennedy felt that he was sitting uncomfortably close to her.

John talked a lot about himself and his band for most of the evening. Kennedy learned that he did have a real day job, working for the Environmental Protection Agency. He told her the story of how he had dropped out of school to become a river-raft guide in Colorado. Then he eventually made it back to Arkansas and finished his degree.

At the end of the date, Kennedy couldn't decide whether she liked him or not. John seemed as if he would be a fun guy. He also seemed very forward. He went in for a heavy make-out session before she got in her car to leave. *This was another Year of Yes date*, thought Kennedy.

THE WAITING GAME

The third Thursday in November, Kennedy flew to Denver for the second time that year. This time it was for a dental conference. Jenna, Bailey, Meredith, and Lauren were all going to be at the conference and were splitting a hotel room downtown. However, Kennedy was staying with Sydney and Trey at their apartment in Cherry Creek.

It stayed around seventeen degrees Fahrenheit that weekend in Denver. Snow was falling lightly off and on the first day there. Sydney and Kennedy spent Thursday night catching up with each other's lives. Sydney was telling Kennedy how she was still anxiously waiting for Trey to propose to her.

"I'm sure it will happen. He's still in school, paying on loans. Also, you guys are living together. So he kind of already has you," said Kennedy.

"But he doesn't have me forever right now. If he doesn't propose soon, I'll feel I'm wasting my time. I mean, I moved to Denver for him. I'm not getting any younger," replied Sydney.

"I realize that, Sydney. But you can choose to just embrace this as an adventure if it doesn't work out."

"I know. I'm just impatient!"

"We spend so much of our time as women waiting for the man to make his move," Kennedy said. "Shouldn't we have some control over our own destiny? I moved for Sam, remember? I thought that it was my fate that he proposed. That was my path. But, it didn't work out. So I chose a new path. Now, here I am, being a single dog lady. I'm alone, and I'm happy with that."

"I'm glad to know you're happy. But I thought you were dating someone. What happened to the Kneeler?"

"I broke up with him. I couldn't see myself marrying him. I found out that he was a smoker. You know I can't handle what cigarettes do to teeth. Also, he told me that he wanted to move to a tiny town in Arkansas and live there for the rest of his life. You know I can't do farm life. But, I did go on a date with a banjo player yesterday," said Kennedy.

"Is this a joke? He plays the banjo for a living?"

"Yes, his name is John. He's short. But he's cute. He has a day job. But, I don't think it's going to work out. He stood on his tippy toes to kiss me. Also, I told Captain Dave that I would be here this weekend."

"Oh! Where is ol' Dave now?"

"He's in Albuquerque. I think it's four hours from here," said Kennedy.

"Oh? Do you think he'll show up?"

"It's undoubtedly too far a drive, and he's probably too busy. I didn't ask. Plus, we haven't seen each other in months."

THE PILOT'S RETURN

The following morning, Sydney dropped Kennedy off at the Denver Convention Center for her continuing education classes. In the middle of her second class, Kennedy received a text from David. The message said that he was driving up from his parents' house in Buena Vista, Colorado. He asked her what time she was getting out of class. Kennedy's heart skipped a beat. She hadn't thought that he would come to visit her.

Kennedy met up with Jenna, Bailey, Lauren, and Meredith by the big blue bear statue at the front of the convention center after their classes.

"We want to go to the Voodoo Doughnut Shop," Jenna told Kennedy.

"I heard it was famous for its doughnuts. I want a doughnut with bacon on it," said Lauren.

"Well, I have a friend in town. He's on his way now. Do you remember me telling you about David, the air force pilot?" asked Kennedy.

"What? I didn't know you guys were still talking!" said Jenna, shocked.

"I didn't either. We haven't talked in a month or two. But he's coming—right now. Let's see if he'll drive us to Voodoo," said Kennedy.

David pulled up in front of the Denver Convention Center in a small four-door sedan that he had borrowed from his mom. Kennedy walked up and opened the passenger door.

"Hello, driver! Do you think you can take us ladies to Voodoo Doughnut Shop?" asked Kennedy. She gave David a wide smile.

David obliged. The five women piled into the small car and headed to get doughnuts and coffee. The roads were snowy, so David drove the girls slowly through downtown Denver. When the car pulled up to the doughnut shop, the four in the back excited the car. David and Kennedy stayed in the car. David moved toward Kennedy for a long hug and a kiss on the cheek.

"I'm so glad I get to see you this weekend," David told her.

"Me too. I'm surprised you made it. It was a good surprise," said Kennedy. She felt a twinge of awkwardness at seeing her lost lover. Yet it seemed as if time had hardly passed at all.

"My mom made you coffee cake," David said as he held up a plastic container.

"That was nice of her. I'll have to save it for later, after the doughnuts," said Kennedy.

The girls and David all huddled in the long line in the crowded little doughnut shop. There was nowhere to sit. David suggested they move to the bar next door.

Jenna told Kennedy that they were going to take the doughnuts back to the hotel. They needed to get ready to go out that night. The four girls called an Uber, leaving David and Kennedy at the little bar next door to the doughnut shop. Kennedy had the bartender make her coffee into an Irish coffee, and David ordered a beer. Their beverages complimented the taste of the delicious doughnuts.

"This city is great. There are so many things to do here! So many young people!" Kennedy said. "I might move. I think I'm ready to get out of Little Rock."

"You should definitely move here! You would have a better social life," said David.

"I would get to hang out with Sydney more. Also, I would be closer to you too," said Kennedy.

"Actually, Kennedy, I'm being stationed back to Japan," said David. He took a giant bite out of his doughnut.

"Really? When do you leave?" asked Kennedy.

"In two months—January."

"Oh, that's soon. How long have you known?"

"For a few weeks now. I thought I would tell you in person."

"Oh, are you excited about it?"

"Yes, I'm more excited about it than I would be about staying in Albuquerque. They're going to retire my model of C-130 soon. If I stay in the States, I would have to learn to fly the new C-130. Then I would probably retire after that. I would rather be beneficial in Japan with the current C-130 because there were fewer pilots in Okinawa with my specialty. Plus, my status as Captain is a little more respected over there than here."

"So, they asked you to go?" asked Kennedy.

"Yes, and I took the offer. Kennedy, a war with ISIS is coming. I'll be able to help more in Japan than in the States."

Kennedy had no idea why that was. But she trusted he was doing the right thing for himself. She wasn't going to stop him.

THE BIG NO

The next day, after more continuing education classes, David and his friend Will led the women on an unofficial beer tour of Denver. They went to the Great Divide, the Vine Street Pub, and the Copper Kettle Brewing Company. The group ended with a drunken tour of the Museum of Money in downtown Denver.

"Sydney and Trey want to watch the Arkansas vs LSU game somewhere. Any ideas?" Kennedy asked David and Will.

Kennedy, Sydney, Trey, Will, and David all ended up at Bayou Bob's to watch the game. Will, who was a Louisiana State fan, suggested the restaurant. To their surprise, the bar was filled with LSU fans.

Kennedy, Sydney, and Trey were all dressed in red-and-black Razorback gear. It was somewhat overwhelming. Fortunately, the Razorbacks won.

After the game, Trey and Sydney left to go to another party. Then David, Will, and Kennedy went to a cigar-and-piano bar downtown. They ordered whiskey drinks and listened to a live jazz band.

"Why do you think Trey hasn't proposed to Sydney? She's a great catch," asked David.

"I think it's because he's still in school. Also, I'm nervous that she's pushing him too much," said Kennedy.

"He's Peter Panning," said Will.

"What?" asked Kennedy.

"He's trying to stay young forever—like Peter Pan. I'm Peter Panning right now. I'm thirty-five and nowhere near ready to settle down," said Will. He was taller than David. His eyes were dark brown, framed by graceful brows. He had high cheekbones, a square jaw and a cleft chin. He was more handsome than David—which, at the time, Kennedy didn't think possible. He was the kind of guy who could get any girl he wanted. But he was waiting for the right one—maybe.

While Will was taking a bathroom break, David scooted closer to Kennedy and put his arm around her.

"If you moved to Denver, you could marry Will," said David.

"What? I'm not going to marry Will," replied Kennedy with a raised brow.

"Then you could move to Japan with me," said David.

Kennedy looked at David and wondered if he was being serious. Will returned from the bathroom. The conversation changed to rock climbing and world traveling.

David spent the night with Kennedy in Sydney and Trey's guest bedroom that night. The next day, he drove Kennedy to the airport. It was a forty-minute drive. Kennedy and David talked the entire way.

Before Kennedy got out of David's mom's car, David kissed her and said, "Think about Japan."

He couldn't make it for just a weekend, thought Kennedy.

The pilot had come and gone again in Kennedy's life. She knew that she loved him, but she couldn't admit to it to anyone. She was too stubborn and afraid of the unknown. She was too afraid of being hurt. Impractical relationships—this was what she gets herself into.

On the plane, she wondered what it would be like to marry the air force pilot. She would be moving with him constantly. She would have to make new friends wherever they went. She would be alone a lot. But she was independent enough now that she would be okay. Also, if she had kids, she would have to find a support network other than her family to help. Especially if David was deployed. Women all over the world bravely lived this lifestyle. She wondered how she would pay off her student loans. She did plan on continuing working as a dentist. Were there dental jobs for Americans in Japan?

No, she thought, *Japan is out of the question*. She could not say yes to this.

12. DECEMBER

December won't you come
Back with snow even sun
Don't say that it's done
I will carry you home.

-Norah Jones

THE DISCONNECT

"Have you thought any more about Japan?" asked Kennedy's mom.

"You think I'm actually considering going?" replied Kennedy.

"Kennedy, it would definitely be a new adventure. He seems like a nice man. Also, he's Catholic. It's very hard nowadays to find a nice Catholic young man."

"I will consider visiting. But Mom, he's going to be there for the next three years. I can't wait that long for him. Also, I can't afford to move away and not pay my student loans."

"Three years is a very long time for you to be away from the United States," her father replied.

"That's true and I've thought of that. Also, I can't move to Japan for a man I've dated for only four months. I moved for Sam. I lived his life. It was all about him. That's exactly what I would be doing with David. I don't think I can give up my life for a man. Not right now."

"For the right person, you would move," said Kennedy's mother.

"Yeah, and you're eventually going to run out of options," said Josh, her loving brother.

"Gosh, you're so right!" Kennedy cried. "I'm turning into an old spinster as we speak! I should move to Japan with a man I dated for four months because that is my only option. This might be my last chance at finding a husband. All you guys worry about is if I will ever find a husband to settle down with." Kennedy was fed up with everyone attacking her singleness.

"Oh, honey, that's not true. We just want you to be happy," replied her mother.

"I am happy, Mom. Please let me live my life without judging it," Kennedy said, looking right at Josh.

It had been a week since David had dropped Kennedy off at the airport and driven back to Albuquerque. He had told Kennedy he had a tough couple of weeks ahead of him in pilot training. He had to buckle down and pass all of his exams if he wanted to graduate from this sector and move on to Japan.

Kennedy was driving from her parents' house in northwest Arkansas to Little Rock. She decided to call David to see how he was doing. David picked up the phone after two rings.

"Hey, I have a lot of studying to get through right now. Can I give you a call later tonight?" said David.

"Yeah, that will work," said Kennedy.

David never called Kennedy back. Later, she learned through a mutual friend, that David's best friend, Mark, had died that day when his fighter jet crashed in the Middle East. Mark had left behind his wife and new baby girl.

David was heartbroken.

CHRISTMAS EVE'S EVE

Every year for the past five years, on the night before Christmas Eve, Kennedy and Piper would attend the Marley's Fund Christmas Concert on Dickson Street in Fayetteville. The band members were guys that Piper and Kennedy had gone to high school with. The money was donated to a favorite charity of one of their classmates who had died in a car accident. Every year, Kennedy and Piper would get severely intoxicated and would take the Boozer Cruiser back to Piper's house.

During the concert, Kennedy received a text message from David.

David: I'm drunk. So forgive me—are we idiots for not being together?

Kennedy: No, you're an idiot for not being with me. I haven't heard from you in weeks.

David: Fair enough. If I asked you to really lay it on the line for me, would you do it?

Kennedy: If I laid it on the line for you, would you lay it on the line right back? I'm looking for an equal, a partner. Someone who will reschedule an adventure to be there for me when I need him. I want to be with someone who is willing to sacrifice for me just as much as I do for him.

David: You are wise. I don't know if I can do that yet.

Kennedy: David, I can't wait four years for you to come back from Japan. Also, I can't come with you. There are so many reasons why I can't.

At this point, Kennedy realized that she couldn't say yes to everything in the Year of Yes. In fact, she hadn't said yes to everything. If she had, she would have said yes to David's drunken marriage proposal in May. Kennedy believed in fate. But she also understood that if she said yes to everything, she would have no control over what she wanted her life to be.

At one thirty in the morning, Piper and Kennedy had the Boozer Cruiser take them to Taco Bell on the way home from the concert. When they got back to Piper's house, Kennedy was hazy drunk to the point where she had the spins. Piper and Kennedy had gotten several free drinks from old classmates at the concert.

It was two o'clock when David called Kennedy.

"Kennedy, did you only go on a date with me because it was the Year of Yes?" he asked.

"How did you know about that?"

"Robyn told me that night at Cajun's."

Kennedy didn't know how to answer this question. It was true that she had gone on a date with him only because of this. Although he was handsome, he was not her usual "type" of guy. They didn't necessarily agree politically or socially.

"Is that why you proposed to me after Cajun's? You thought I would automatically say yes?" she asked.

"No...I...I don't know."

"I did go on the second date with you because of the Year of Yes. It's the reason we're even talking right now. Yes...Yess...Yess...It's so exhausting." Kennedy was drunk and chattering over the phone.

"If this year was the Year of Yes, what is next year going to be called?"

"The Year of...Meh," Kennedy replied with a shrug.

"Kennedy...the reason I didn't call you back. It's been difficult for me lately. Mufasa was hit by a car last week."

"What? How did that happen?"

"He was staying with my parents in Colorado. My best friend, Mark, died at the beginning of December. His fighter jet crashed in the Middle East. So I flew to South Korea to escort his body the rest of the way back to the United States. While I was gone, Mufasa got out of my parent's back yard and ran into the street and was hit by a truck. They couldn't save him."

There was long silence over the phone.

"My offer for Japan still stands. I want you to come with me. You would be an amazing wife and travel companion."

"I'm so sorry about your loss, David. But I can't move to Japan with you. Not right now." Kennedy hung up the phone.

She was drunkenly sprawled out on her back in the middle of Piper's kitchen floor. Tears rolled down her cheeks and off of her chin. She had her cell phone in one hand and a chicken soft taco in the other. Piper found her at this moment and picked her up off the floor. Piper took the soft taco out of Kennedy's hand and gently led her to bed. Kennedy hadn't even said good-bye to David.

NEW YEAR NEW YOU

I t was December 31, New Year's Eve. Kennedy and Piper flew back to Denver to celebrate New Year's with Sydney and Trey. Kennedy and Piper knew the entire night that Trey had a ring in his pocket and was ready to propose to Sydney.

It was close to midnight. Kennedy was swaying to the music of the band. To her right she saw Trey go down on one knee to propose to Sydney. She looked to her left and locked eyes with a handsome stranger. He walked toward her through the crowd as the countdown to the New Year began.

Five...
"Will you make me the happiest man alive and marry me?" Trey asked Sydney.

Four...
"Can I kiss you on the cheek?" the stranger said into Kennedy's ear.

Three...
"Yes," replied Sydney. She was crying tears of joy and jumping up and down.

Two...
"Yes," replied Kennedy to the stranger, who gave her a kiss on the cheek.

One...
Kennedy blinked, and the Year of Yes was over.

Looking back on the year, she realized that she had accomplished several feats that she hadn't in her previous life – being alone, meeting strangers, running (half of a half) and public speaking to name a few. She had grown up and grown into her own skin. She had forgiven Sam and left behind her feelings of guilt and loss that they didn't work out. It was as if, in leaving Sam, she had woken up from a stupor of dependency. She felt stronger and more confident. She knew she had made the right decision to leave. She had made the right decision to say yes to the men she had dated, they all taught her something about herself. She had made the right decision saying no to David and moving to Japan.

Kennedy was also feeling ready and able to open her heart again to new love. However, she wasn't one hundred percent sure that David was the one. At this very moment, she was no longer worried about rushing to find a man or finding the "perfect" one. Kennedy was confident that she would continue living a fulfilled life regardless of whether she found the perfect love or not. However, she also knew that she might not find the perfect love in Little Rock.

So in the very early hours of the New Year, Kennedy made a decision to say yes to one more thing: moving away from Little Rock.

I was told to go
Where the wind would blow
And it blows away-away

--Alabama Shakes

LETTER FROM THE AUTHOR

Dear Readers,
The original title of this book the was the Year of Yes. Unfortunately, the wonderful and forever inspiring Shonda Rhimes jumped on that title and published her book before I could even get my masterpiece edited. Apparently, we were having a Year of Year around the same time. She is much more successful than I am. I am not angry about her accomplishments and her *New York Times Bestseller* label. Especially since I have watched and loved everything she's ever done. Also, this is my debut novel and I'm self-publishing. If anyone actually reads this book, I will be ecstatic.

Love,
Annie Powers
P.S. There might be a second book and maybe even a third. Keep an eye out ;-).